HORSES OF

Half Moon

RANCH

WILD HORSES / RODEO ROCKY

JENNY OLDFIELD

Illustrated by
Paul Hunt

Hodder
Children's
Books

a division of Hodder Headline Limited

Also by Jenny Oldfield
published by Hodder Children's Books

WILD HORSES

JENNY OLDFIELD

Illustrated by
Paul Hunt

Hodder
Children's
Books

a division of Hodder Headline Limited

This edition of *Wild Horses* and *Rodeo Rocky* first published in 2000.
ISBN 0 340 792302

Wild Horses

With thanks to Bob, Karen and Katie Foster, and to the staff and guests at Lost Valley Ranch, Deckers, Colorado

Visit Jenny Oldfield's website at
www.testware.co.uk/jenny oldfield

Copyright © 1999 Jenny Oldfield
Illustrations copyright © 1999 Paul Hunt

First published as a single volume in Great Britain in 1999
by Hodder Children's Books

A catalogue record for this book is available from the British Library

Typeset by Avon Dataset Ltd, Bidford-on-Avon, Warks

Printed and bound in Great Britain by
The Guernsey Press Co. Ltd, Guernsey, Channel Islands

Hodder Children's Books
a division of Hodder Headline Limited
338 Euston Road
London NW1 3BH

1

Kirstie Scott felt the bounce in Lucky's stride. His head was up, ears flicking to left and right as she relaxed in the saddle and gave him plenty of rein.

'Let's head for Miners' Ridge,' Charlie Miller called from the front. He reined his horse to the right and led the group of seven riders along a narrow trail between silver aspen trees.

Great! Kirstie smiled to herself and nudged Lucky on with her legs. Miners' Ridge, at the end of Meltwater Trail, was one of her favourite treks out from Half-Moon Ranch. It would take them by the banks of rushing creeks and waterfalls, through spooky Dead Man's Canyon.

Good! Lucky echoed her mood by picking up his pace. He broke into an easy trot, splashing through a shallow stream to catch up with Charlie and tuck himself in behind Moose, the young wrangler's sturdy grey quarter horse.

Behind them, the other six riders took things more slowly. It was the last Saturday in May; their first day as paying guests at the Scotts' ranch. To them, the steep slopes leading through dark pine forests and beyond that to snow-peaked mountains, were new and risky.

'You gotta trust your horses,' Charlie assured them. 'They know the trail. All you gotta do is stay in line.'

Kirstie grinned over her shoulder at the nervous followers. They were visitors from cities and towns, mostly without much riding experience. Trust your horse; that was the key. With a creak of saddle leather, she turned back and gazed straight ahead.

Sure, it looked difficult. The trail rose sharply, zig-zagging between boulders, overhung by branches. But it looked pretty too. The bright green aspen leaves shook and fluttered in the breeze, a carpet of blue columbines grew around the roots. Summer! Kirstie sighed. After the long, cold Colorado winter of snow and ice, the leaves and the flowers were just great.

Summer was here and school was out. 'Good boy, Lucky!' she murmured as her beautiful palomino picked his way between boulders. His rich golden coat looked dappled in the fluttering shadows, his long, creamy mane hung smoothly down his neck.

No more school through June and July. And her mother had driven to Denver this very morning to pick up Kirstie's big brother, Matt, from college. The family would be together again. Long days to ride the trails. Blue skies and mountains rolling on forever . . .

'Kirstie?' Charlie broke into her dream.

'Hmm?' She sighed, pushed a wisp of fair hair back from her face, then urged Lucky alongside Moose.

'Can you lead? I need to check on that guy at the back of the line.'

'The one who's riding Silver Flash?' She glanced back at the last rider. The middle-aged man had decided to leave the trail and take a short cut to the front. He'd forced his sorrel-coloured mare off the track and shoved her up against a rocky slope which was impossible for Silver Flash to climb. Now he was digging his heels in hard, grunting and leaning forward in the saddle to make the horse go. 'Sure,' Kirstie told Charlie, as the wrangler went off to sort the man out.

She and Lucky went on with the rest of the group, a woman with two teenage sons, and a young married couple. Up ahead, the trail hit a short, level, sunny patch before it climbed again, this time between the tall, scaly trunks of ponderosa pine.

'This sure is tough going,' the woman behind her remarked as the gloomier trees closed in.

She was riding Johnny Mohawk, a dainty, sure-footed black horse that Kirstie had helped her mother to buy last fall. Kirstie nodded but said nothing.

'I sure do hope the weather holds,' the woman went on, an edge of nervousness in her voice.

4

Kirstie glanced up. There were glimpses in the distance of clouds gathering over Eagle's Peak; at 13,000 feet the highest mountain around. 'Yep,' she agreed.

'What happens if it rains? Do we turn back and head for the ranch house?'

'Nope.' Kirstie didn't like to talk much while she rode. She preferred silence; to hear the stiff, dry rustle of the pine needles as the wind drove through the trees, to breathe in the sharp woody smells and look out for chipmunks or ground squirrels scurrying on ahead of the horses' plodding feet.

So she was glad when Charlie came back up front. 'I tell you one thing for sure,' he muttered in Kirstie's ear as he rode by on Moose. 'Some horses are much smarter than your average dude.'

She grinned back at him. 'Silver Flash is a pretty smart horse,' she agreed, pleased to see that horse and dude rider were back in line. She and Charlie often shared a joke. He was 19 years old, a year younger than her brother, Matt, and had come to work at Half-Moon just after Christmas. Tall and dark, with cropped, black hair, he wore a thick, big-checked blue and white shirt, worn-out jeans and battered cowboy boots.

'How long before we reach Miners' Ridge?' the nervous woman on Johnny Mohawk asked now, one eye still on the distant rain clouds.

Charlie rode Moose steadily on, waiting to answer until after he'd helped his horse pick his way across a splashing stream. Then he turned in his saddle and yelled over the sound of the water. 'The whole ride should take us three hours or thereabouts.' Pointing to the track of the stream, he showed them where he planned to lead them. 'See there, up by the fall? The trail heads off to the left, up to Hummingbird Rock. And past that, you see where the two cliffs meet in a narrow pass?'

The group of visitors scrunched up their faces, peered up the hill at the rocky horizon, then nodded.

'That's Dead Man's Canyon. We get through there, up on to the ridge until we come across the opening to an old goldmine. And that's when we start heading for home.' Charlie grinned, then reined Moose to the left, on up the slope.

It was Kirstie's turn to take Lucky through the

racing stream. She leaned back in the saddle as he strode down the bank, heard the clunk of his hooves as they hit the rocky bed. The white, foaming water splashed up around her boots and jeans. 'Trust your horse.' She heard Charlie's advice inside her head and let Lucky find his own way across. The palomino's hooves slid and clunked, found solid ground, trod safely on. Ten seconds later, they were through the stream and climbing up the far bank.

Ten *minutes* later, after much urging and encouraging from Charlie, the six visitors had also made it.

'A little wet around the ankles,' Johnny Mohawk's rider, Loretta, complained. 'But worth it!'

She smiled at Kirstie and Kirstie smiled back.

'You know something?' Loretta confided as the group rode on through the ponderosas towards Dead Man's Canyon.

'Nope,' Kirstie replied, swinging her hair behind her shoulders with a quick toss of her head.

'I never thought I'd say this when we first came on the trail. I mean, I was pretty darned scared back there . . .' She settled into her saddle, tucked in behind Lucky, heading for the tall, grey cliff faces that formed the narrow canyon.

'Say what?' Kirstie glanced back at the slight, pale-faced woman with short, dark hair. Her face was excited and kind of lit up at having crossed the tricky stream. There was a light in Kirstie's own large, grey eyes. She'd just guessed what Loretta was about to confess.

'This week here at Half-Moon Ranch; I think it's gonna be a whole lot of fun!'

Fun and tons of hard work for the family who ran it, Kirstie thought. She settled back into listening to the wind in the trees as she ended her talk with Loretta and rode on.

Kirstie had left the city and moved here with her mother and brother just four years ago, when she was nine years old. 'Here' was at the end of a five mile dirt road off Route 3 out of San Luis, a small town of one main street, a grocery store and a gas station, which was another ten miles down the paved road. 'Here' was 8,000 feet up in the Rocky Mountains, in the Meltwater Range, and it was uphill all the way to Wyoming. Fifteen miles to school each day; three and a half hours by car to Denver, where she'd once lived.

That had been when her dad had still been part of their family, and her grandma and grandpa had run Half-Moon Ranch, grazing a few hundred longhorn cattle in the green valley by Five Mile Creek.

Then, in one terrible year, when she was eight, it had all fallen apart. Her dad had left home suddenly; almost, it seemed to Kirstie, without a word of warning. One day he was there, driving into his office in the city. The next day, the Good Friday before Easter, he'd packed his bags and gone, leaving a hole where he'd once been, an empty place at the table, a space in the garage, no one in the big double bed beside her mom.

Matt, Kirstie and Sandy Scott. No Glen Scott. Their dad had a new girlfriend, a new life. His picture was in the silver frame on the bookshelf. That was all.

That weekend they had driven out to Half-Moon Ranch to be with Grandma and Grandpa. Kirstie's mom had gone around the log-built ranch house in dazed silence, while Kirstie and Matt rode out with Grandpa to bring in some early calves. It set the pattern for that first, lonely summer; driving out of town at weekends, away from the emptiness of their Denver home, to a place where nothing ever changed.

Only it did. Kirstie had just turned nine when, sudden as her dad's leaving, Grandpa fell ill and died of a heart attack. And this time she didn't even have a chance to say goodbye. The old man had been out working the cattle. It was their farmhand, Hadley Crane, who came riding back to Grandma with the news.

They called out the doctor from San Luis, but by the time he got there it was way too late.

People at the funeral said it was how old Chuck Glassner would have wanted to die: suddenly, out working the cattle by the side of Five Mile Creek. That puzzled Kirstie: she knew her grandpa would never have wanted to leave his ranch, his wife, his daughter and grandchildren – he loved them all too much.

But now, four years later, she was beginning to understand. She ran through those years as the shadows of Dead Man's Canyon began to close down on the small group of horses and riders. She remembered the day when they'd shut up the neat, modern house in Denver and moved out to Half-Moon Ranch for good.

Sandy Scott had decided to take the gamble of leaving the city with her two kids and setting up home and business on the eastern slopes of the Colorado Rockies. With Grandma's blessing, they were going to turn the cattle ranch into a small vacation centre for paying guests. There were five cabins to build in the aspen trees that sheltered the original ranch house; small log houses with open fires, sitting-rooms and bedrooms where visitors would be comfortable.

That took a year of hard work from Hadley and another cowhand, who had stayed on after Grandpa's death. Then there were horses to buy at the horse sale barn in San Luis – Hadley again, though by this time Sandy herself had developed a good eye for the points of a horse. She planned ahead, bought wisely, waited for Hadley and a couple of local men to build a sound corral, strong tack-room and feeding-stalls.

Then, two summers ago, Half-Moon had finally opened its doors to paying guests.

Kirstie took a deep breath at the memory of her mom's face as she'd welcomed their first visitors. It had been nervous, with small frown marks between her fair eyebrows, and she'd been too brisk in showing them to their cabins . . .

Just then Lucky tensed beneath the saddle, picking up his rider's momentary edginess. His ears flicked round, quizzing Kirstie. What's the problem? Was it something I did?

'Not you,' she murmured. She clicked her tongue gently against the roof of her mouth to urge him on. 'It was me. I was just . . . thinking.' She sighed again.

The winter before last had been her grandma's time to fall ill. In Kirstie's mind, the old lady seemed to fade with the light. As days grew shorter, nights longer and colder, and the aspen leaves had turned from bright gold to brown, her gran had grown more frail. This time there was no surprise; Kirstie knew she would die.

'I've seen you build this place from nothing,' Grandma had told Sandy in her last days. 'I've seen you work and build a whole new life out here. I'm so proud.'

She had slid away from them, died peacefully, and Kirstie's sadness, though strong, was less sharply painful than at the other two terrible times.

These things had made her quieter than she was before, less likely to rely on people being there for her when she needed them. And now, when she looked at her mom and the growing success of the ranch, she could believe that a person could make anything happen, if only they wanted it enough. It made her feel good . . . That, and the horses of Half-Moon Ranch.

Lucky, Moose, Johnny Mohawk and Silver Flash. Crazy Horse and Cadillac, her brother Matt's favourite. More than a dozen horses of all colours: sorrel, fleabitten grey, palomino and Appaloosas; all good American quarter horses, but each with their own personality and special spirit.

Like Silver Flash now; the sorrel horse with the bright white flash down the length of his bony, intelligent face. He knew all too well that he had a complete beginner on his back. The man was heavy, with a dark moustache. His name was

Ronnie Vernon and he worked at a bank in Dallas, Texas. Whenever he tried to dig his heels into Silver Flash's sides to make him break from the line and trot forwards, the smart horse refused to obey.

From up front, Charlie caught sight of Ronnie Vernon's tactics. He sighed and asked Kirstie to head the line once more. 'Don't try to overtake as we get near the canyon!' he yelled at the man, turning Moose and heading down the slope to make sure that his instructions got through.

Meanwhile, Kirstie knew there was another stream to cross before the horses could enter the narrow channel between the rocks into Dead Man's Canyon. Horseshoe Creek was coming up; she could hear the water gushing and tumbling down the rocks around the next bend in the trail.

'Sounds kind of full,' Loretta said, still following close on Lucky's heels.

'That would be the snow melting from the mountain tops,' Kirstie explained. 'It all runs down into Five Mile Creek and on into Big Bear River. This time of year there's always a lot of water.'

She and Lucky rounded the bend first, to find

the creek leaping and swirling its way between wet black rocks. It tumbled over tree trunks that had fallen across its path, and sent white spray drifting towards them.

'Wow!' One of Loretta's sons pulled Cadillac to a sudden halt. The big, creamy-white horse tossed his head and skittered sideways. Back down the line, everyone stopped.

'It's OK. Follow me.' Kirstie had made this crossing dozens of times before, and she knew the safest place. It was only the wild sound of the water surging between the rocks that made it seem more difficult than it really was.

Lucky knew this too. He went boldly forward to the water's edge, dropped his head, and with his ears pricked forward, stepped into the fast-running stream.

Kirstie's horse was strong and certain. She knew he would pick his way through. And she loved the feel of the ice-cold spray on her hands and face as Lucky steadied himself, then went on, picking up his feet to step over a fallen log, letting the torrent push against his sturdy legs without giving way.

'Good boy!' Kirstie leaned forward to pat his

neck as Lucky stepped up the far bank. Now they must wait for Loretta to pluck up the courage to try. 'Come on, it's fine!' she called back. 'Give Johnny Mohawk his head and let him do it for you!'

She watched the dainty black horse put a first foot in the water, and noticed that, right at the back of the line, Charlie had finally got Ronnie Vernon in order.

The wrangler gave her a wave and yelled at her to go ahead into the canyon. 'We'll meet up with you there!'

So Kirstie watched Loretta through, then urged Lucky on, glad to let Charlie take charge once more. And she picked up an eagerness in her horse too. He seemed to be in a hurry, putting more pace into his walk. She clicked and he broke into a trot. 'What is it?' she murmured. 'What have you heard?'

Lucky's ears were forward, his head up, as they entered Dead Man's Canyon. A wind whipped through his pale mane and his golden shoulders grew dark with sweat as they left the group behind.

'You heard something,' Kirstie acknowledged, tensing a little. Or was it just the wind and the

16

darkening sky that had made Lucky quicken his pace? Those distant clouds over Eagle's Peak were speeding towards them, drawing down on to Miners' Ridge, bringing rain. 'Easy, boy!' she whispered, holding him back from a lope.

The rocks to either side rose sheer and blocked what was left of the sun. The shadows closed in.

And then she saw.

Lucky stopped dead. And Kirstie discovered what it was that had made him so eager to push ahead.

A herd of horses had gathered at the far end of the canyon. Horses without headcollars, their manes tangled, heads up, tails swishing a warning to the intruders. Beautiful sorrels, dazzling greys, paints and Appaloosas. Horses that had never been broken to wear bridle or bit.

Wild horses. And at their head, watching every move that Kirstie and Lucky made, was their leader. Taller than the rest, with a proud, arched neck and flaring nostril, the black stallion kept guard.

'Easy!' Kirstie whispered to Lucky. The wild horses had penned themselves into a dead end where the walls of the canyon finally met. The only way out was by a steep trail to her right, up on to Miners' Ridge.

The horse was perfect and proud, strong and fierce as he pawed at the ground to warn them away from his herd. His black coat shone, his mane fell forward over his long, wild face.

Holding her breath and not daring to move, Kirstie stared in silence at the beautiful black stallion.

Unflinching under her gaze, the proud horse stared back as the dark clouds rolled towards them, and in the distance, over Eagle's Peak, forked lightning flashed.

2

The stallion stared back at Kirstie and Lucky. His herd milled restlessly in the stony gulley where Dead Man's Canyon came to an abrupt end. Sheer red-brown cliffs towered above them, trapping them. He studied the two possible escape routes; the trail which Kirstie had travelled, or the steep track up the cliffs to Miners' Ridge.

Striking the rocky earth with his front hoof, the stallion tossed his head. He swung angrily towards Lucky, then turned his head and trotted back, corralling his herd deeper into the impassable gulley.

'Easy!' Kirstie breathed. Behind her, Charlie calmed the other trail horses and their uneasy riders. She could feel Lucky's flanks quiver, saw his ears flatten against his neck. A rumble of thunder rolled overhead, setting the palomino's ears still further back. He stepped sideways, tugging at the reins in fright.

Then there was more lightning, this time just above them. A great, forked flash of it tearing through the dark clouds. And drops of cold rain, large and slow at first, spattering on to the rocks and the trapped horses.

Lucky flinched at the electric flash. Thirty metres from where he and Kirstie stood, the black stallion reared. He went up on to his hind legs, his front feet flailing, head back, teeth bared. Another blinding flash, and this time the thunder rolled across the ridge with a clatter and a crack. A wind drove the clouds down the snow-topped mountain in a torrrent of icy, hard rain.

'Come on, let's get out of here!' Kirstie decided to veer away from the hostile stallion and his frightened herd. In the flashing lightning and crashing thunder, it must seem to them that she and Lucky were blocking their escape. So she reined Lucky to the left, hoping to leave the way clear for the wild horses to reach the track on to the ridge.

But then, before the stallion could pick up her good intention, there was the sound of more hooves drumming behind them. A blurred shape appeared in the rain at the mouth of the canyon; a man on horseback galloping at full speed.

Surprised, holding Lucky on a tight rein, Kirstie peered through the sheet of rain. She made out the heavy figure of Ronnie Vernon on Silver Flash. The horse was out of control, no doubt spooked by his clumsy rider and by the storm into stampeding ahead of the rest of the group. Clinging to the saddle horn, his jacket flying open, hatless and soaked, Vernon careered towards her.

For a few stunned seconds, Kirstie thought they were headed for a collision. Rapidly she sidestepped Lucky out of the runaway horse's path, heard the wild stallion whinny from the depths of the gulley. Lucky whirled on the spot, testing her balance to the limit.

Then Silver Flash made a decision of his own. He'd spotted the track on to Miner's Ridge. It was a trail he knew well, so he headed for it, regardless of his rider. It was his only way out of this echoing, dark, storm-torn place and he took it.

Steadying Lucky, Kirstie stared after them. Silver Flash's hooves drummed up the narrow track, setting small stones rolling. It was the route she'd wanted the stallion to use, but now the wild herd cowered at the far end of the canyon once more, away from the falling stones. Meanwhile, the rain bounced off the rocks and formed muddy brown streams in the dirt channels, loosening more stones.

'Kirstie!' Charlie's voice yelled from the mouth of the canyon. 'Don't let that rider go any further. It's not safe!'

'Too late!' she yelled back.

Vernon and Silver Flash were fifty metres up the slope, now dislodging bigger stones that crashed over the edge of the track and landed on the canyon floor. One missed the black stallion by less than a metre. He reared up and sideways as it crashed down, his wet mane straggled across a neck that was flecked with white spots of sweat.

'Then look out for yourself and get out of there!' Charlie called. He'd ridden after Vernon as far as the mouth of Dead Man's Canyon and taken in the scene through the sheet of rain; Kirsty and Lucky to one side, the wild herd at the far end, and the cliff track crumbling under Silver Flash's hooves as Vernon rode him high on to the ridge.

'What about the wild horses?' she cried.

'Never mind them. Just get out as fast as you can!'

Behind Charlie, Kirstie made out a huddle of riders. He was right; she had to get out quick. The sooner she and Lucky left the canyon, the easier it would be for the black stallion to lead the herd out too. So she kicked Lucky into action. For some reason he wouldn't go. She kicked again.

'Get a move on!' Charlie shouted, his voice hoarse.

'I can't! Lucky won't shift!'

More rocks fell; bigger and louder, crowding the wild herd against the wall of the canyon. Overhead, Silver Flash was scrambling up the last stretch of track on to the ridge.

Kirstie was soaked to the skin, rainwater running

from her scalp, down her face, dripping through her shirt on to her shoulders and back, drenching her jeans. 'Come on, Lucky, please!'

Nothing. He stood like the statue of a horse in the eye of the storm.

And then, as if in slow motion, the lines and contours around her changed shape. The actual land shifted. Only Lucky stayed still as every inch of rock tilted and slipped.

'Landslide!' Charlie yelled, as if from a great distance. Then his voice was swallowed by the roar of falling rock.

Landslide! The cliff face where Vernon had raced his horse on to the ridge was crumbling. Whole chunks of brown rock were breaking away and tumbling, caving in like sugar under a deluge of muddy water. Uprooted trees swayed and toppled in a din of snapping branches, a blur of green and brown.

Gasping, almost crying, Kirstie pulled Lucky tight into the opposite cliff. No wonder the poor horse had refused to move. He'd sensed the landslide before she had and kept to the only safe place in the canyon.

The rock fall gathered momentum. The cliff face cracked and disintegrated as a flash of lightning lit up the whole terrifying scene; horses cowering as rocks crumbled and crashed, the black stallion driving them back as they tried to make a crazy dash towards the disappearing cliff.

Still Lucky was frozen with fear. If they stayed in this spot now, a tumbling rock would soon get them. Kirstie decided she must jump off and lead him out of danger.

Throwing her leg over the back of the saddle, she slipped from Lucky's back, grabbed the reins and tried to move him out of danger. There was still time to do as Charlie had said and head for the mouth of the canyon. But they had to be quick. She tugged at the reins and sobbed. 'Come on, Lucky, please!'

Muscles locked, legs planted wide, he refused.

And the rocks kept on coming. They were sliding in muddy heaps, piling up across the exit, blocking their way.

Lucky strained back from the reins, eyes rolling. It was no good; Kirstie couldn't shift him.

Alone she could make it. If she dropped the

reins and scrambled through the debris, she could get out of this death-trap. But it would mean leaving Lucky. She would rather die than do that. Really, she would rather die.

Instead of abandoning her beloved horse to his fate, she dropped the reins and circled her arms around his neck. 'OK,' she sighed. 'You win. We wait here until it's all over.'

'You OK in there?' It was Charlie's voice, muffled by the rockfall that blocked the entrance to Dead Man's Canyon. Other anxious voices backed him up, demanding to know how Kirstie was.

The silence after the shattering crash of rock against rock was eerie. All she could hear was the rain pattering down. Kirstie opened her eyes. 'We're fine!' she called back. All in one piece. No bones broken.

That was a miracle in itself. After she'd thrown her arms around Lucky's neck and waited, the rocks had kept on coming. She'd heard them bounce and splinter, split off in every direction then land with sickening thuds. But not one had touched them or even left a scratch.

'How about Silver Flash?' Charlie asked.

She stared up at the new shape of the cliff. It had jagged chasms, streams and waterfalls where there had once been trees and a thin covering of earth. The fleeing horse and his novice rider were nowhere to be seen. 'I don't know!' she replied in a faint, scared voice.

'Listen, Kirstie; we can't get over this fall of rock to reach you! It's too high, and pretty dangerous by the look of things.' Charlie sounded worried despite her assurance that she and Lucky were OK. 'How is it on your side?'

She took a deep breath and dragged her gaze away from the ragged, uneven ridge. Her eyes swept quickly down the altered rock-face, along the canyon to the narrow gulley. It was difficult to make out shapes in the dust and drizzling rain, but there, at the far end, the herd of wild horses stood in petrified silence. 'Not too bad,' she called to Charlie. 'Except the track up on to the ridge has gone, so it looks like there's no way out.'

'OK.' Charlie obviously needed time to think it through.

There was more silence. Then Kirstie noticed

27

what she should have spotted straight away. She looked again, through the gloom at the group of ghostly horses. 'There was a wild horse in here; a lead male!' she cried to the listeners beyond the landslide. 'Charlie, the black stallion's gone!'

The shock tore into her. One moment he'd stood there, his black coat streaming with rain, wide-shouldered, deep-chested. His long tail had swung, his feet had stamped. He was protecting his herd. Next moment, the land fell away. Now he was gone.

Had she imagined him? Was he a shadow against the red cliff, a figment of her imagination? Perhaps no real horse could ever have been so perfect.

Kirstie laid a hand on Lucky's neck. He dipped his head and nudged her forward. Then he too took a step across the rock-strewn canyon.

The horses in the wild herd saw them move. They edged nervously away, around the rim of the gulley, all looking grey and unreal through the rain. Ignoring them, Lucky put his head down and headed ten, fifteen metres towards a heap of newly-fallen rocks. Two uprooted pine trees had landed in the shape of a cross beside the unstable pile,

their branches brushing the ground and making a green screen in front of the crumbled cliff face.

Trust your horse. It was the golden rule at Half-Moon Ranch. Lucky knew what he was doing. So Kirstie stepped after him, right up to the screen of broken branches and sharp pine needles, where the palomino had stopped. Pushing past him, she climbed up the heap and pushed the nearest branch to one side.

Her heart lurched again. There, half buried beneath the rockfall, was the stallion.

Kirstie let out a gasp. Straight away, before she could even think, she squatted down and began tearing at the fallen rocks with her hands, heaving them to one side, wrenching with all her might. The horse was motionless, eyes closed, head sunk awkwardly against a ledge, his front legs invisible, but his back legs and hindquarters clear of the landslide.

If she could just move the rocks from his chest and shoulders . . . She tore away, grazing her hands so badly they bled. The scarlet trickles merged with the rain and mud, but she didn't feel the cuts. All that mattered was freeing the stallion.

He was unconscious, but still breathing. She could see his chest heave as she dragged a large rock free. But what about his legs? She went more carefully now, lifting the last rocks from around his girth until she uncovered the long, black front legs. Then she stopped and sat back on her haunches, staring down at a blood-soaked mess. The horse's left knee had been crushed by a heavy rock.

'Kirstie?' Charlie's voice drifted over the barrier of boulders and mud.

She swallowed hard, struggled to control her voice. 'I've found him!'

'The stallion? Is he hurt?'

'Yes.'

'Bad?'

'Pretty bad. Charlie, we need help!' Softly she put out a bleeding hand to touch the stallion. She stroked the soaked black coat, wiped away the dirt from around his mouth and nostrils.

The horse opened his eyes. They flickered shut, then opened again. He lifted his head.

'Easy!' she whispered.

Lucky stepped back to give the wild creature space.

The stallion pulled away from Kirstie's hand. His eyes rolled in fear at the human touch.

'It's OK,' she whispered. 'I won't hurt you.'

But he didn't trust her. He lay on his side, kicking with his back legs, feebly at first, then more strongly as he regained consciousness. He wanted to be up, away from the pile of ugly rocks that had crashed down on to him, away from the girl with bleeding hands, her soaking hair plastered to her skull, her face smeared with mud.

Kirstie held her breath. She wanted to help him on to his feet and he wouldn't let her. Instead, he struggled alone. He got his back legs under him, ready to take his weight and shove. His head was raised. Now his knees should bend and he should roll from his side on to them, then push up until he was standing. But his injured knee buckled under him. Once, twice, he tried but sank back.

'Charlie, fetch help!' Kirstie stood up, took hold of Lucky's reins and together they ran towards the debris that blocked the entrance. 'I don't care how you get in here, just fetch help . . . please!'

'OK. I'll radio to base and take the whole group back to the ranch with me. You hang on, do what you can for him!' The wrangler took the only way out of the mess.

'Don't be long!' she pleaded.

'About an hour and a half,' he promised. 'Just hang on, OK?'

Dragging breath into her lungs to stem the panic that almost choked her, she convinced him that she would be OK. 'Go, Charlie!' she cried.

An hour and a half before anyone came . . . Would her mom and Matt be back from Denver? Could they get the vet over from San Luis? If they did, would the wild stallion let him near? And were his injuries too bad to treat?

Questions crowded into her head and jostled for answers. None came. Meanwhile, as the herd waited uneasily by the far cliff and Lucky stood patiently at a distance, Kirstie knew that it was up to her to calm the injured horse and stop the bleeding from his injured leg.

She turned to face him, his life in her hands.

3

The stallion knew that he was helpless, his magnificent power stripped away by the crashing rocks. As Kirstie went cautiously towards him again, anxious not to distress him, his whole body quivered. His eyes rolled, his nostrils flared.

Behind her, Lucky followed then came to a halt midway between the injured horse and the rest of the herd. His metal shoe struck bare rock and echoed through the canyon making the wild horses shy away in a tight huddle. Without their leader, trapped by the landslide, they turned and swung nervously this way and that.

'Easy, boy!' Kirstie whispered as she approached the bleeding horse.

He was struggling to raise himself, pawing at the ground with his front feet, reaching out his head and straining to take his weight on the injured knee.

'Wait!' Kirstie drew near. She knew horses and some basic first aid, so she planned what to do. The first thing was that the wound needed to be strapped tight to stop the bleeding. If the stallion would let her get close enough. Breathing steady, reassuring words, she advanced step by step.

The horse tossed his head, whipping his wet black mane back from his face. He watched her every move.

If she looked him in the eye, he would see this as a threat, Kirstie knew. So she kept her gaze fixed on the wounded knee. She inched towards him, her eyes averted, murmuring encouragement.

The stallion struggled again, every nerve straining against her approach.

When eventually she was within a few inches of

him, feeling his hot breath on her hand as she knelt and stretched out to touch him, slowly, slowly winning his trust, she decided on her next move.

She was wearing a T-shirt under her denim shirt so, quickly and smoothly, she withdrew her hand and unbuttoned her top shirt. It was soaking wet from the rain, but once she had it off, she was able to pull hard at a seam and tear down the length of one side. Within a minute, the pale blue shirt was in strips, ready to use as a bandage around the stallion's knee.

The horse's head was up, his eyes watchful, his body still quivering with tension and pain. The clink of a bridle and the sound of metal shoes shuffling over rocky ground in the background told Kirstie that Lucky was still wisely keeping a safe distance.

'Here we go!' she breathed, taking one end of the makeshift bandage and edging forward on her knees. Luckily the stallion's left leg was uppermost, the damaged knee clearly on view. Kirstie flinched as she saw the skin scraped back from the bony joint, the jagged, dirty wound and the steady flow of blood on the wet rock where he lay. But she pressed on, determined to lay the bandage across the wound and slip the fabric under the leg so that she could begin winding it and strapping it tight.

'Good boy!' she soothed. Amazingly, a sixth sense must have told the wild creature that she was offering him his only chance of survival. He kept his head up, watching her as she strapped the wound, but he didn't resist.

Kirstie worked quickly. When one length of torn shirt was used up, she began another. At first, blood seeped quickly through each layer, but then the tight padding began to take effect. Soon, the bleeding eased and she was able to secure the bandage in a tight knot.

Taking a deep breath, she sat back on her haunches. Now it was important to get the stallion on his feet. If he stayed down until help arrived, he would lose heart. He had to get up under his own steam. Yet how was she going to help him stand? She looked round, searching for the right idea.

The herd was still milling around in the gulley. Lucky was waiting nearby. If she borrowed his headcollar and halter rope, which the Half-Moon horses sometimes wore under their bits and bridles, she might have the solution.

So she slipped quickly to where Lucky stood and, with hasty fingers, fumbled with the wet straps and buckles. At last she slid the headcollar off and unhitched the halter rope from the side of the saddle horn. Then she ran back to the black stallion.

'Now trust me,' she urged, offering him the headcollar. Of course, he'd never seen anything like this before. Would he take it quietly or resist?

The horse's head drew back from the contraption. Through his pain and confusion, a deep instinct told him that the headcollar was not to be trusted. This was a trap.

'Not for long!' Kirstie whispered. 'I promise!'

With one hand on his neck, she used the other to ease the headcollar towards his soft, grey nose. Again he jerked away. Kirstie insisted. She took her hand from his neck and offered the collar with both hands. This was going to be the only way.

The more the stallion leaned away, the firmer

she became. She urged the collar on to him, talking quietly, easing the straps over his nose and under his throat. Since he couldn't move from the spot where he'd fallen, in the end he had to accept.

The collar was on, buckled tight. The rope trailed across the rocks. The horse shook his head, ears back, hating the feel of the straps.

Getting to her feet, Kirstie judged the best move. It was the left leg that was injured. It now stuck straight out, stiffened by the tight strapping around the knee. But the right knee looked sound. What she had to do was to use the collar and rope to persuade the horse to rise to his feet, taking his weight on the right leg only. So she went round to his right side, carrying the rope, bringing his attention round to that side.

He followed her with his deep brown, intelligent eyes. As she tightened the rope and raised it, he seemed to understand. With his back legs he shifted his weight the way Kirstie intended. He kept his left front leg straight and bent his right leg under him.

'That's great. Good boy!' Kirstie held her breath. If he could get up, if he could be on his feet by the time Charlie came back, she reckoned he stood a chance.

The stallion fought to keep his balance. He was pushing with the sound front leg, but it was a lop-sided movement that he'd never made before. He felt the halter rope tug his weight to one side, whinnied with pain as for a moment he tried to bend the strapped and injured knee.

The horses in the gulley heard the cry and broke apart, trotting wildly in different directions down the length of the canyon.

'Try again!' Kirstie whispered to the horse, pulling hard on the halter rope.

He pushed. His back feet found the ground, his legs straightened and he tipped forward on to the sound right knee. Kirstie pulled on the rope. Up, up!

And he made it at last, whinnying at the pain in his left knee, swaying as he rose, until he was up on his feet, towering over Kirstie, straining at the rope and pulling away from her.

'Easy, easy!' She tried to hang on. But once more the horse was powerful. Yes, he stumbled when he tried to put weight on the injured leg, but he was fighting her now, wrenching the rope from her hands. It burned her palms as he tugged free.

She gasped and let go. The horse had trusted her only so far. Now he was up and wild again, snaking the halter rope through the air in an effort to rid himself of the hated headcollar.

And the herd was gathering, waiting by the main rock fall to see what their leader would do.

Over their heads, along the ridge from the direction of the ranch, more horses were approaching. As the stallion stumbled off to join

his herd, trailing the rope, Lucky trotted up to Kirstie to let her know that help was arriving.

But the sound unnerved the wild horses even more. Hooves thundered along Miners' Ridge at a gallop, and they were trapped with a wounded leader in a canyon from which there seemed no escape. As Charlie and Hadley Crane appeared at the head of the gulley, the herd reared and wheeled in frantic efforts to find a way out.

'Kirstie!' Charlie raced along the edge of the canyon yelling her name. He stopped Moose and leaped from his back, coming to the edge of the cliff face. 'Your mom's not back from Denver, but Hadley here called her on the phone.'

The older man dismounted more slowly and joined him. 'She says to get you out of there!' he called, crouching alongside Charlie. His grey stetson was pulled well down over his weather-beaten face, and he was dressed in fringed leather chaps that covered the fronts of his legs, over his jeans. In spite of the recent storm, he wasn't wearing anything more waterproof than a battered denim jacket.

'But what about the stallion?' Kirstie cried.

Hadley's gaze followed the crazed path of the wild herd up and down the canyon. He saw the wounded leader limping to the far end, trailing the rope that Kirstie had attached. 'Your mom's trying to get in touch with Glen Woodford in San Luis,' he told her. 'She'll tell him the problem, then he can deal with it. But she said not to take no for an answer; she wants me to get you home!'

Kirstie groaned. Glen Woodford was the nearest vet, but it sounded like he might be out on another job. 'I don't want to leave the stallion!' she protested, tilting her head back and cupping her hands around her mouth so that Charlie and Hadley could hear.

'I got my orders!' Hadley hollered back. He began to look round the steep cliffs for a possible way out for Kirstie. 'Ain't nothing you can do about the injured horse.'

'Looks like you did plenty already!' Charlie added. He'd spotted the pale bandage around the stallion's leg. 'You got him up on his feet, didn't you?'

'But he needs me here!' Kirstie stepped quickly to one side as a grey mare split off from the herd and thundered down the canyon towards her. A distant rumble of thunder had spooked her and sent her on a crazy sprint.

'Listen, if you don't do as your mom says, I got orders to come down there and fetch you out!' The old ranch hand's gravelly voice reached her over the thudding hooves. 'You gotta climb out right now, and Charlie and me will get you back to Half-Moon Ranch before the boss arrives!'

'What about Lucky?' Leaving the wild horses trapped here was one thing, but she couldn't ever think of going home without her palomino.

There was silence as the two men scanned the cliffs.

'You could try leading him out!' Charlie yelled. 'There ain't a track no more, but Lucky's smart. He can help you find a way up to the ridge!'

More horses thudded by, churning up mud and splattering it over Kirstie's already soaked jeans and T-shirt.

'Yep, try that,' Hadley agreed. 'Don't ride him, though. It ain't safe.'

Kirstie pushed her hair back from her forehead and glanced at the stallion. 'He needs a suture in the gash on his leg!' she told them. 'Maybe his knee's even broken; I can't say.'

'Leave that to Glen!' Hadley grew impatient. 'Anyhow, if it's that bad, there ain't no point losing sleep wondering how to get him out, is there?'

She knew that the old wrangler was saying in so many words that a horse with a broken knee would have to be shot. Her heart thumped against her ribcage and she couldn't answer.

'Are you coming up or are we coming down?' Charlie demanded, standing hands on hips at the edge of the cliff.

There was nothing else for it; she and Lucky would have to abandon the wild horses to their fate until the vet from San Luis arrived. In any case, Glen Woodford would probably call at the ranch before coming up to Dead Man's Canyon, so Kirstie calculated that the best thing to do would be to be there to explain. 'We're coming!' she yelled, taking the palomino's reins and looking for any likely path to climb.

As they trod carefully through the debris of rocks left by the landslide, and with the lightning flashing in the bruised blue sky over distant Eagle's

Peak, she kept one eye on the stallion. He was still on his feet, but his head was down, his left leg lifted off the ground. Then he shook his head from side to side, making the halter rope flail through the air.

'Wait here,' she told Lucky, making another quick decision. Then she shouted up to Charlie and Hadley. 'He hates the headcollar; I want to take it off before we leave.'

'You sure?' Charlie queried.

'Yep. I promised.' 'Not for long' was what she'd told the horse. Even if it helped the vet when he eventually got here for her to leave the collar on, how could she break her word and leave the rope swinging from the hated harness?

So she dropped Lucky's reins and moved in quickly on the stallion, almost before he was aware. The rest of the herd beat a retreat, and she was able to catch hold of the rope, ease in, unbuckle the strap and slip his head out of the collar in one swift move. The black horse reared away, then stumbled on to his injured leg. But she'd freed him according to her promise. He limped away and joined the herd.

'Get a move on, Kirstie!' Hadley insisted. He pointed down at Lucky. 'Your horse is showing you how!'

Sure enough, Lucky had set off by himself up the steep, rocky slope. Surefooted as ever, he eased himself over boulders, testing for loose stones and taking a sensible route towards where the two men stood.

Kirstie scrambled after him. For the first time since Ronnie Vernon's reckless race out of the canyon on Silver Flash, she realised how tired she was. Her legs felt heavy and stiff, her cut hands began to throb as she hauled her way up the steep slope.

Half way up, Lucky stopped to wait in the thin drizzle that was still falling. Kirstie caught him up.

'You OK?' Hadley checked.

She looked up and nodded.

'Just follow the horse,' the old man insisted.

On they went. Sometimes Lucky would misjudge his footing and a stone would break loose and fall. Sometimes it would be Kirstie stretching for a handhold that held them up.

'Don't look down!' Charlie hissed as she neared

the top of the ridge. He caught hold of Lucky's reins as the horse finally made it. Handing them to Hadley, he reached down again to haul Kirstie up the final stretch.

'Don't worry, I won't!' She knew about the dizzying drop into the canyon without having to look. She was glad for the strength of Charlie's arm as he lifted her to safety.

And then she did turn and gaze back the way they'd come. With Lucky breathing hard beside her, and Hadley hurrying them along, she paused.

'What do you think? Is his leg broken?' she murmured to Charlie, who was staring down at the herd of wild horses, taking one last look.

The young wrangler shrugged. 'Best leave that to Glen Woodford.'

'I hope it's not.' She watched the stallion limp to the far end of the canyon surrounded by his herd. He was moving around; that was good. But he was bending down to nip at the makeshift bandage, trying to scratch and bite at it. It looked like it wouldn't be long before he managed it, then perhaps the bleeding would start afresh. Kirstie sighed helplessly.

'Let's go,' Hadley insisted, already astride his horse and handing Kirstie her reins.

Kirstie mounted Lucky. A numbness threatened to set in the moment the horses began to move away along the ridge, but she fought it off. She had to stay clear-headed to explain to people back at the ranch exactly what had happened. Glancing up, she saw that the rain clouds over the far-off mountain still hadn't cleared.

So she turned in the saddle to catch a last glimpse of the black stallion. He looked up at the departing figures on Miners' Ridge. 'We'll be back,' she promised.

Her voice was lost in a dull roll of thunder, her face pale and drained under the latest flash of forked lightning in the stormy sky.

4

'I know how much you care about this injured horse, but you don't go anywhere or do anything until you've changed your wet clothes,' Sandy Scott told Kirstie.

'But, Mom . . .'

'No buts.'

'But . . .'

Sandy grabbed her by the shoulders and turned her to face the stairs. 'Scoot! Go on up and find some dry things!'

Kirstie felt herself shunted upstairs. Matt gave her a grin in passing, and flung a towel at her. The grin said, 'Better do as she says!'

As she got rid of Kirstie, Sandy spread her hands in a gesture of helplessness. 'I turn my back for a single morning, and what happens?'

'You can't blame the kid for a landslide!' Matt protested. 'Even Kirstie couldn't stop a mountain collapsing on her!'

'But if there's trouble around, she'll find it.' Sandy didn't bother to lower her voice as she got busy in the big ranch-house kitchen, putting coffee on the stove and finding mugs for Charlie and Hadley. 'How come it was Kirstie who went up Dead Man's Canyon ahead of the rest?'

'That was down to me,' Charlie admitted, his own voice quiet and subdued. 'I had a small problem down the line.'

'It wasn't Charlie's fault!' Kirstie yelled from her bedroom. She pulled open drawers and turfed out dry shirts until she found the one she wanted. She changed, then gave her fair hair a rapid rub with the towel. Where in the world was Glen Woodford? She'd arrived at the ranch after half an hour's weary ride to find her mom and brother, but no sign of the vet.

In double-quick time she was changed and taking the stairs two at a time to join the others.

'These wild horses; where do you reckon they came from?' Sandy was asking Hadley Crane.

The wiry old man shrugged. 'I did hear tell of a herd up by Eden Lake a week back.' His slow voice drawled over every word. He was standing, hat in hand, with his back to the wood-burning stove. His jacket steamed, his leather chaps were still tied firmly round his long legs.

'And these are the same ones?'

'Could be. From what I heard, no one got close enough to take a proper look.'

Kirstie listened hard. She knew that Eden Lake was way up above 10,000 feet. The winter snow would still be on the ground, lying in the rock crevices and covering the mountain tops. The meadows between the peaks would only just be beginning to show green. It made sense that if the wild herd had been spotted up there, they would since have moved down the mountains for better grazing.

As she figured it out she felt her brother, Matt, sidle up to her. 'Watch out; one lecture coming up,' he warned.

'From Mom?'

Matt nodded. 'She was real worried.'

'I was OK. It was the black stallion I was thinking about.'

'Yeah!' he grinned. 'So tell me something new!'

Kirstie blushed as Matt teased her about her obsession. 'What would *you* have done? Found him under a pile of rocks and just left him?'

'Nope. I'd have done about the same as you, I guess.'

This time she grinned back. She and Matt didn't look alike; he was tall and dark, where she was middle-sized and fair. He had light hazel eyes like their dad, hers were soft grey like her mom's. Everyone said Matt was good-looking, the image of his absent father. 'Beautiful but dumb,' their mother would joke with a touch of regret.

But even though they looked different, Kirstie knew that her brother shared her love of horses.

'So how's the stallion?' he asked her now. All he'd heard so far was a garbled story told in snatches by Charlie as Matt had helped him unsaddle the horses in the corral.

'Lost a lot of blood,' Kirstie reported. 'The cut on his knee's real bad and real dirty. I guess he needs a tetanus shot and antibiotics.'

'Charlie thinks maybe his leg's broken?' Matt said quietly, as their mom went on to discuss with Hadley the chances of shifting the pile of rocks that blocked the entrance to Dead Man's Canyon.

Kirstie shrugged and turned away. Only Glen Woodford would be able to tell them that. For now, all they could do was wait. And for Kirstie, waiting was hard.

'That's a mighty big landslide back there.' Hadley scratched his head where the hair grew short and iron-grey. 'I reckon it'll take some serious earth-moving equipment to pull that pile of rocks away.'

Charlie nodded. 'It's the only way to get the stallion out of there,' he reminded them. 'No way can he do what Lucky did and climb out by himself.'

Sandy Scott chewed her lip as she thought it through. Dressed in shirt and jeans like the men on the ranch, but slight and feminine under her workmanlike clothes, she wore her fair hair pulled loosely back. Her young-looking face was tanned from working in the clear summer sun, but it was creased right now by a worried frown. 'The problem is, we still have a ranch to run,' she reminded them. 'Finding equipment to move the rocks and rescue this horse sounds like it's gonna take a whole lot of time.'

This was where Matt stepped in. 'Let me take over from Hadley and lead one of the rides this afternoon,' he suggested. 'That leaves one man free to go back to Dead Man's Canyon.'

Hadley grunted, then nodded. 'I reckon I could get over to Lennie Goodman's place at Lone Elm and borrow his JCB. If I get the go ahead, I could drive the machine along Meltwater Trail and start work.'

'Let me come!' Kirstie joined in. Lone Elm was a trailer park a couple of miles along the creek. The owner, Lennie Goodman, used the big yellow tractor-type vehicle with a giant metal scoop across the front to shift earth and make new sites for the big trailers and recreational vehicles that visited the area.

Sandy glanced at her watch. 'The guests are over in the dining-room having lunch. We have half an hour before the afternoon rides. If we all lend a hand to saddle up the horses, I reckon Hadley and Kirstie could take the afternoon off.'

'Great!' Kirstie jumped in, taking her mom at her word. She headed for the door, jamming a baseball-cap on to her head, urging Hadley to hurry.

But the old man never did anything in a rush. He said he would ring Lennie Goodman to check things out, sending Charlie after Kirstie across to the corral to help prepare the horses for the afternoon ride. Soon Matt and Sandy joined them there too.

Kirstie went from horse to horse along the tethered row. She checked their stirrups and tightened their cinches after Charlie and Matt had lifted the heavy saddles across their broad backs. When she came to Silver Flash, however, she saw that the big sorrel horse stood in his headcollar, without saddle or bridle.

'Ronnie Vernon won't be riding this afternoon,' Charlie told her. 'He says he wants to go fishing instead.'

'Hmm.' She wrinkled her nose, then sniffed. Personally, after the way he'd disobeyed orders and raced Silver Flash up out of the canyon this morning, she wouldn't care if the man never rode again.

'He feels pretty bad,' Charlie reported.

'Tell me about it.' She raised her fair eyebrows until they disappeared under the peak of her cap. A glance towards the dining-room showed her the man himself walking quickly in the other direction, away from the corral. 'You could say he was the reason the stallion got hurt.'

'You mean he started the landslide?' Matt frowned.

Sandy stopped work to listen.

Kirstie untethered Silver Flash, ready to lead him out to the ramuda, the strip of grassland by Five Mile Creek. 'He's the one who set the first rocks sliding by making his horse lope up the track.'

'Yeah, but there was a lot of rain coming down that ridge.' Charlie stepped in to remind them that Vernon shouldn't take all the blame. 'The water loosened the whole thing up. It could've happened to anyone.'

Sandy nodded, giving Kirstie a meaningful look. 'Let's leave it, OK?'

Kirstie blushed, realising that she might be being hot-headed. She was worked up by vivid memories of the injured horse. 'Sorry,' she said quietly.

'No, it's OK, I understand.' Her mom walked alongside as Kirstie led Silver Flash down to the meadow. 'They tell me you fixed the stallion up pretty good.'

'Let's hope.' She recalled her last view of him, angered by the bandage around his leg, trapped in the canyon as more rain clouds rolled down the mountain.

'You did a good job, Kirstie.' Sandy watched her daughter put Silver Flash to graze, then stretched an arm around her shoulder.

'I wish Glen Woodford would get here!' Try as she might, she couldn't get the main problem out of her mind: the first-aid treatment she'd given the badly injured horse wouldn't hold out for long. What the stallion really needed was a vet. And quick.

But she was distracted by the sight of a new figure riding on a bike down the dirt track from the main gates of Half-Moon Ranch. She recognised the short red hair and long limbs of her best friend, Lisa Goodman. Lisa was Lennie Goodman's grand-daughter, the same age as Kirstie and in the same grade at San Luis Middle School.

'Hey!' Lisa spotted Kirstie and Sandy and veered across the grass towards them. 'I was at Lone Elm when Hadley called!' she explained, flinging her bike down. 'He told us what happened.'

'Can your grandpa lend Hadley the earth-mover?' Kirstie asked.

'Sure. He's driving it over from the trailer park right now. I came on ahead.' Breathless from her ride, Lisa walked back to the corral with Kirstie and her mother. 'Sounds like you got a real problem on your hands,' she gasped. 'Can I come see?'

Quickly Kirstie nodded. She knew Lisa wouldn't be in the way. 'Hadley can take over and drive the JCB when your grandpa brings it. We'll saddle Cadillac for you . . .'

'Best ask Matt first,' Sandy reminded them. 'He's back home now, remember!'

'Ask me what?' Matt came out of the tack-room to catch the end of the sentence. He'd taken off his college clothes and wore his stetson and riding-boots instead, ready for the afternoon's work. 'Does someone want to borrow my horse by any chance?'

They arranged with him for Lisa to ride Matt's white gelding, and while they were doing this, a black Jeep rode down the track to the ranch house.

'Glen Woodford!' Kirstie cried, breaking away from the group. She climbed the corral fence and ran to meet him. 'What kept you?'

Ignoring her question, the vet jumped down from the Jeep, slammed the door and strode towards her. 'Hey, Kirstie, I hear you can put me in the picture. How's this injured horse of yours doing?'

As she explained, Charlie went out to the ramuda to fetch yet another horse, this time for the vet. The wrangler said they should ride across country to the canyon to save time. 'Dirt roads round here are flooded,' he told them. 'According to Lennie, Five Mile Creek broke its banks.'

Glen nodded and went to fetch his bag from the

car, while Kirstie ran for a saddle-bag for him and strapped it on to the back of his horse's saddle. Meanwhile, Lisa was up on Cadillac, ready and waiting.

'You got a two-way radio with you?' Sandy asked, as Kirstie mounted Lucky.

She nodded.

'Keep us in touch. I'll be out leading the beginners' ride.' Sandy glanced round to see the first guests leaving the dining-room and heading for the corral.

Glen Woodford promised to keep an eye on both girls. 'We should reach the canyon before Hadley gets there with the JCB,' he guessed. 'According to Kirstie, I should be able to climb down from the ridge. If it goes well, I can treat the horse's injuries, give him a couple of shots of Procaine, and be out of there before the work on moving the rocks begins. Then it'll be up to Hadley to make a way out for the whole herd.'

'Let's go!' Impatient to set off, her hopes raised by the vet's confident words, Kirstie tapped her heels against Lucky's sides.

The willing palomino strode out across the

corral, followed by Lisa on Cadillac and Glen on a brown and white six-year-old paint called Yukon.

'Forget the trails!' Kirstie called over her shoulder, heading Lucky straight up the slope behind the ranch. 'We'll bushwhack across country; it'll be quicker!' She calculated roughly forty-five minutes to the canyon, caught a glimpse of the giant yellow earth-mover trundling slowly along Meltwater Trail as they rose high through the aspen trees. Overhead, the clouds still threatened, but for the moment the rain held off.

Three-quarters of an hour of pushing the horses uphill, picking their way clear of the lime-green aspens into the darker, spikier ponderosa pines. Silent except for the occasional snorting of the hardworking horses, the three riders concentrated on finding the quickest route to Miners' Ridge.

'What's this Procaine shot you mentioned earlier?' Lisa asked Glen as they climbed the final slopes. Though she lived at a diner in town with her mother, Bonnie Goodman, and didn't ride as often as Kirstie, she'd kept up well.

'Procaine is a type of Penicillin,' the vet explained. 'And the stallion will need one big dose of tetanus, since these are wild horses we're dealing with and there's no chance of them being immunized already.'

'And will you stitch the wound?' Lisa quizzed.

Glen shrugged. 'Don't know yet. Sutures don't generally hold if the laceration is across a joint. I may be able to give him something to keep down the swelling; let's hold on and see what we find when we get there.'

Kirstie listened without breaking her own silence. The other two were talking as if the stallion's leg wasn't broken, she realised. She hoped they were right.

She let Lucky pick his way up the steep hill, ducking to avoid branches, keeping her weight slightly forwards in the saddle. Soon they would reach the ridge. Noticing Lucky's ears prick forward to listen, she motioned for Glen and Lisa to keep quiet.

'Are we almost there?' Lisa called after a minute or two of now silent progress.

Kirstie nodded. They were coming to mounds of waste stone, long since grassed over; stony relics left by the goldminers way back last century. They would dig deep into the mountain with dynamite and picks, haul the rock out to the mine entrance and dump it before burrowing back deep into the earth. During one bad winter a big explosion had killed many miners, and the accident had given the nearby deep gulley its name. Beyond the rough mounds the long, narrow ridge that overlooked the canyon began.

'That's weird.' Kirstie tilted her head to one side. Like Lucky, she'd been listening hard. 'I can't hear anything.'

Glen Woodford rode up alongside. 'So? What should we hear?'

'Hooves,' she explained. Earlier that morning, the wild horses had made a lot of noise as they pounded up and down the canyon. Now all was silent. 'Really weird!'

'Maybe they're resting.' Lisa looked for an explanation. 'Or listening to us sneaking up on them.'

They rode on until they reached the top of the ridge and were able to look down.

Still no noise. No restless shifting of hooves, no nervous whinnies echoing from the cliffs. Nothing.

'Empty!' Kirstie gasped.

No mares and foals huddled together, jostling down the far end of the gulley.

'How come?' Lisa stared at the blocked entrance where the fallen rocks towered, seemingly too high for a horse to climb.

Kirstie slipped from the saddle and crouched by the sheer drop. 'I don't know!' she breathed. Her hands gripped at the edge of the cliff as she peered down.

The canyon was deserted. There wasn't a living thing down there. But how could a whole herd of wild horses have escaped? And the biggest question of all; where in the world was the injured black stallion?

5

'Where in the world?' was a good question. This out-of-the way place with its unhappy history and its recent sudden disaster was starting to feel like it wasn't in the real world after all. Maybe Kirstie had got it wrong, had imagined the storm and the landslide, the black stallion and the wild herd; maybe she'd dreamed them all.

'Weird!' Lisa echoed Kirstie's uneasy doubts.

Glen Woodford got down slowly from Yukon, pausing to unstrap the saddle-bag and bring his vet's kit with him. He came and crouched at the edge of the ravine beside Kirstie and Lisa, hunching his broad shoulders inside his dark green jacket. 'What do we reckon?' he asked, calm as ever.

Kirstie shook her head. 'They were here!' she insisted. 'And there was no way out!'

Lisa stood up and walked a few steps along the ridge to peer down the canyon from a different angle. 'Zilch,' she reported in a flat voice. 'Big round zero.'

'OK, you guys, let's get this clear.' The vet looked Kirstie straight in the eyes. His square, even-featured face beneath the neat dark hair was serious but showed no sign of irritation. 'This is the right place?'

This time Kirstie nodded. 'For sure. You can ask Charlie.' No way could she have mistaken the canyon.

Glen considered things. 'So maybe the herd climbed out after you left.'

'Maybe.' She was prepared to admit it was possible. 'If they watched Lucky and me pick a new way up to the ridge, I guess they could have got the idea and followed.'

She pictured the dozen or so horses tackling the difficult route.

'But there were foals?' Glen asked. 'The mares would have a tough time leading them up the cliff.'

'I know.' Kirstie sighed and appealed to Lisa for a bright idea.

Lisa looked sideways out of her green eyes, then turned away, muttering.

'Well, maybe. But what beats me is how this injured stallion made it out.' The vet stood up and gazed around, as if the answer to the mystery might be across the far side of the canyon, or further up the mountain. 'You say the leg was real bad?'

'OK, listen. Number one, he was knocked unconscious by falling rocks. Number two, he lost a lot of blood.' Kirstie grew desperate to convince them. 'That means he would be weak. And number three, the knee was so bad I thought it might even be broken!'

Glen took this in. 'So the good news is, you were wrong.' He went on in response to her blank look. 'The knee wasn't that bad . . . not broken, so he found he could put his weight on it and follow the other horses up the track.'

'In other words, he made it out of there on his own?' Lisa got the idea. 'Which means he's doing OK.'

Taking a deep breath, Kirstie nodded slowly. 'I guess.'

'What else?' The vet invited any other explanation. '. . . Which means he didn't need my help after all,' he said after a long pause.

Kirstie felt her face grow hot and flushed at the idea that she'd dragged Glen Woodford all the way from San Luis under false pretences. 'I'm real sorry,' she stammered.

'Don't be.' He smiled kindly, returning to Yukon to pack his vet's kit back into the saddle-bags. 'This kind of happy ending I *like*!'

'So, what we do now is radio a message through to your mom with the good news, then get back to the ranch in time for one of your brilliant cowboy cookouts!' Lisa quickly looked on the bright side. She glanced up at the lightening sky and unzipped her yellow waterproof slicker. 'Saturday. Cookout day. What's to eat?'

'Hmm?' Reluctant to leave the ridge, Kirstie still stared down into the empty canyon. 'I got another idea,' she said slowly.

Lisa came close. 'How come I get the feeling I'm not going to like this so-called idea?' she asked, gingerly crouching down beside Kirstie.

Through her continuing worries about the stallion and her puzzled surprise at finding Dead Man's Canyon empty, Kirstie managed a grin. 'Because it doesn't involve supper at Half-Moon Ranch?' she quipped.

'What's with the "we"?' Lisa demanded as she stood by Cadillac's side and waved Glen Woodford and Yukon off down the mountain. 'You told your mom that "we" wanted to camp the night by Dead Man's Canyon!'

She made Kirstie laugh with her over-the-top expression of disgust. '*We* want to find the stallion, don't we?'

'Yeah . . .'

'And *we* like sleeping out in summer?' She'd persuaded her mom that it would be great for her and Lisa to make camp up here.

'What will you use for a tent?' Sandy had asked over the two-way radio. 'And what will you eat?'

Kirstie's answer had been that Matt could ride up to the ridge before supper with the camping gear and food for both the girls and the horses.

Sandy Scott had thought about it, then asked her to hand over the radio to Glen Woodford for his opinion.

'They'd do fine,' the vet had told her with a wink at the girls. 'No problem!'

So it had been fixed. Kirstie and Lisa were sleeping out.

A message had been sent to Hadley that the earth-moving equipment wouldn't after all be needed right away. The wrangler had turned around and begun to head back to Lone Elm trailer park. And Matt had, as expected, been easygoing about bringing supplies when Sandy had reached him by two-way radio.

'Great, Mom. Thanks!' Kirstie had clicked off the radio just as the vet had been ready to leave. Now she too waved and wished him a safe journey back to the ranch.

'So . . . ?' Lisa watched Glen disappear down the slope, then took off her slicker, rolled it and stuffed it into a saddle-bag hitched to the back of Cadillac's saddle.

'So, we wait till Matt gets here with the feed for Cadillac and Lucky. Then we pitch the tent and cook beans and burgers . . .'

'Yuck!' Lisa pulled a face.

'You said you wanted a cook-out!' Kirstie reminded her.

'Yeah. I was thinking more like chicken, marinated and grilled over an open fire. Baked potatoes, coleslaw . . . the full works. Not beans!' Lisa's face was comically disappointed.

'So . . . cowboy-up!' she told her with a big grin. It was the Scott family's motto, half-jokey, half-serious. 'It's tough, but you know we can do it!'

Lisa rolled her eyes again and pretended to sink against the rough bark of the tall pine tree. 'There you go with that "we" thing again!' she sighed.

The small, dome-shaped tent was up. Beans were cooking on the tiny stove.

'You don't find it kinda . . . spooky up here?' Matt mentioned as he gave Lucky and Cadillac their feed.

'Nope!' Kirstie said with lightning speed.

'Yep!' Lisa shot back.

'To me it feels like this place never gets the sun,' Matt went on. 'It's kind of shadowy, reminds me of, well, spooks, I guess.'

'Thanks, Matt!' Kirstie muttered. Lisa was already jittery enough, without him putting his size ten boots in it.

'Oh, don't . . .' Lisa stared around at the lengthening shadows. A breeze in the trees rattled branches. Some small creature, a chipmunk or a ground squirrel, scuttled off through the bushes.

Matt smiled to himself. He waited until Lucky had finished feeding, then let him wander off to a safe distance to chew on a small patch of new grass. 'All those dead miners,' he reminded them in a ghostly voice. 'Lost in the rush to grab gold from the mountain. Killed by greed!'

'Yeah, that was way back,' Kirstie insisted. 'You're talking centuries here.' Nevertheless, she did glance up from the stove towards the grassed-over mounds of waste from the old mines.

Lisa followed her gaze. 'What's that?' She pointed with a shaking hand about fifty metres up the hill to what looked like a cave between the mounds.

'That's an old mine entrance.' Matt saw she was hooked on his story. 'I guess it goes pretty deep; a black hole into the heart of the mountain! A scar on nature left by man's lust for gold!'

Kirstie jumped up from stirring the pan. 'Don't listen to him,' she told Lisa, striding over to Matt. 'He's winding us up.'

'Me?' His eyes were still smiling. 'Would I?'

'Yes, you would!' Kirstie turned him around and marched him back towards Moose. 'Go home, Matt!'

Swinging into the saddle, laughing out loud, he prepared to do as he was told. 'So why the camp?' he asked before he left. 'Why here? Why now?'

'Because!' Kirstie refused to answer. She stood, arms crossed, looking up at him, waiting for him to go.

'Because she wants to find the black stallion.' Lisa spelled it out. 'Because she can't believe he got out of there alone, without help. She thinks he's still around here some place, needing her.

And you know Kirstie; once she gets a notion, she just won't let go!'

'Promise me one thing,' Matt had insisted before he finally agreed to leave them alone on Miners' Ridge. 'You won't climb down the canyon looking for the horse before daylight.'

'It's a deal.' Kirstie knew he was right. Trying to find a way down was too risky in the gathering dusk. The plan was for her and Lisa to climb into their sleeping-bags the moment it grew dark, get as much sleep as they could, then get up at first light the next morning to continue the search.

'So who can sleep?' Lisa said now that Matt had finally gone. They'd finished the chores, made sure that Cadillac and Lucky were safely tethered and crawled into the tent for the night.

Kirstie was still crouched by the entrance, looking and listening. Except for the rustle of wind through branches and the occasional screech of an owl, the mountain was silent. Ignoring Lisa's question, she went on with her own train of thought. 'If you figure it out, even if the stallion did get out of the canyon somehow, there's no way he can have gone far. He'd be too weak from losing so much blood . . .'

'What was that?' Hearing a new noise, Lisa dived deep into her sleeping-bag and pulled it up round her chin.

'. . . And if he's weak, maybe another stallion in the herd will take over from him as leader and guide the others some place else. That means the black stallion gets left behind. And you know there are mountain lions on Eagle's Peak . . .'

'Lions?' Lisa squeaked. Her head disappeared into the sleeping-bag so that only her curly red hair showed in the glow from the lamp which hung from the roof.

'And black bears. The bears are no problem to the stallion. But a cougar's different.' Kirstie knew that, though rare and seldom seen, a mountain lion would attack a horse weakened by injury. 'They hunt at night,' she told Lisa in a worried voice.

'Don't tell me!' Lisa pleaded.

'So you see, we need to get up at dawn and be out on the trail looking for clues.' She thought ahead, oblivious to the trembling heap inside the sleeping-bag next to her. 'Say we do pick up a track and find him. Say he's weak and all alone. We can stay with him, radio Mom at the ranch, and she can fetch Glen back to give him the shots he needs.'

'Sure,' Lisa said faintly.

Zipping up the tent, Kirstie turned and sighed. She switched off the lamp and threw the tent into complete darkness. 'See, since he didn't get those antibiotics he could be in pretty bad shape by now.' Wearily she crawled fully dressed into her own sleeping-bag. 'In fact, Lisa, I know Glen was trying to make out things looked good for our sakes, but if you really think about it, it's pretty clear to me that the horse could actually die!'

'Help! . . . Help me!'

Rocks crashed down from the roof of a dark tunnel. Dust rose. Men choked and cried out. One picked himself up from the ground and staggered away, arm raised to shield his stooped head from the falling debris.

'I can't get out! I'm trapped! Somebody, help me!'

Voices wailed in the thick blackness. Wild eyes,

anguished faces under a landslide of heavy rocks.

Kirstie beat her fists in the air. Her legs thrashed inside a confined space. 'Help!' she cried, sitting bolt upright.

'Wake up!' Lisa was shaking her. 'You're having a nightmare. Kirstie, wake up!'

She opened her eyes, made out the dome of the tent in the grey light before dawn. Her legs were trapped inside the twisted sleeping-bag, but there were no rocks, no miners suffocating in a dusty tomb. She took a deep breath and, for a few seconds, hung her head forward and buried her face between her hands.

'Are you OK?' Lisa waited until she looked up again.

Kirstie nodded. 'Sorry I woke you.'

'You didn't. I was already awake, looking out for mountain lions . . . bears . . . ghosts . . .' She gave her friend a wry grin. 'Didn't spot any, though. But wait till I see your brother!'

Shaking off the nightmare and reaching out to unzip the tent for fresh air, Kirstie spied Lucky and Cadillac standing quietly under the nearby trees. Both horses looked pale and unreal in the morning mist as they stretched their tethers to turn their heads at the sound of the zip.

She crawled out on all-fours, feeling the cold dew on the grass. Lifting her hands to her hot face, she cooled herself down.

'You're sure you're OK?' Lisa followed her out, already dressed in shirt and trousers.

'Yep. Glad to be awake,' Kirstie confessed. Sleeping out was usually more fun than this, with a saddle-bag full of potato chips and Hershey bars for breakfast, and sun breaking through the trees. Today there was no sun; just more clouds and the wet mist clinging to the ridge. From somewhere deep in the canyon, she recognised the sound of a bobcat's yowl.

Cadillac skittered sideways at the noise. He knocked into Lucky, who tossed his head and pulled at his tether.

With her stomach still churning from the nightmare, Kirstie stood up. Down below, lost in the mist, the bobcat went on making his high-pitched racket. 'I wonder what got into him?'

'And the horses.' Lisa glanced nervously towards Dead Man's Canyon, then over at Lucky and

Cadillac. 'You know something? I'm not the only one who doesn't like this place.'

'I agree. What do you say we saddle up and get out of here fast?' Kirstie suggested, eager in any case to begin the search for the black stallion.

She was heading towards Lucky when a grey shape came hurtling out of the canyon and along the ridge. About a metre long from head to the tip of its stubby tail, with a mottled coat, there was no mistaking the sturdy bobcat. He flew towards Kirstie, saw her and veered off for the trees where the horses were tied up.

It all happened in seconds; the bobcat flashing by, Cadillac smelling and hearing him before he saw him, the wrench at the halter rope, the brittle branch snapping.

'Watch out!' Lisa yelled a warning, too late.

The branch which tethered the two horses had broken. Cadillac reared, dragging Lucky off-balance. The branch cracked and splintered, fell apart, leaving the startled horses free to gallop.

Kirstie stood by, helpless, as the bobcat swerved, then darted between Lucky and Cadillac. Their flailing hooves crashed down inches from where he ran. Then he was clear, darting through the trees out of sight.

'Easy!' Kirstie cried.

Cadillac reared again. A fragment of branch swung from the end of his rope. It crashed against Lucky and sent the palomino prancing towards the edge of the canyon. From higher up the hill, the bobcat gave out his eerie yowl.

Twisting and rearing, sliding and kicking in their efforts to free themselves from the dangling ropes, Cadillac and Lucky ignored Kirstie's call. The mist swirled around them as they struggled. It disguised the sheer drop into the canyon, swallowed first Cadillac's pale, bucking shape, then Lucky's.

Rooted to the spot, Kirstie and Lisa heard a shower of loose stones rattle over the edge of the cliff. The sound of metal shoes on granite rang out.

Then Lucky whinnied, and the sound seemed to unlock Kirstie from her frozen position midway between tent and trees. She jerked into action, sprinting for the cliff, praying she and Lisa would be able to guide Lucky and Cadillac away from the lethal edge.

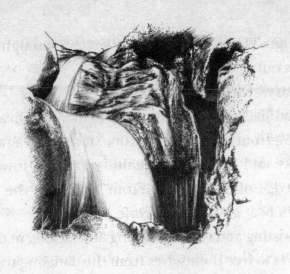

6

'It's OK, Kirstie, I've got Lucky!' Lisa was there before her. She'd seized the palomino's halter rope and held tight, as Kirstie ran through the wet mist.

Kirstie saw a dim outline. Lucky tossed his head and reared, only a few metres from the cliff. When he came down, he ducked, then kicked out with his hind legs, narrowly missing Cadillac behind him. The white horse skewed sideways, away from the edge.

'Easy, Lucky, easy!' Lisa got things under control.

She steadied the frightened horse, leaned into him and pushed him out of danger while Kirstie changed direction and went after Cadillac, disappearing once more into the mist.

'Steady.' She found the big horse standing by one of the mossed-over mounds of waste from the old mine and approached carefully, speaking in a low voice. 'The bobcat's gone. Nothing to be scared about any more.' Privately, Kirstie wasn't so sure. She wondered what had upset the cat in the first place and sent him scooting from the canyon.

'Have you got him?' Lisa called anxiously.

Cadillac had come to a halt at a distance of four or five metres. He eyed Kirstie warily, nostrils flared, one hoof pawing the ground. 'Good boy.' Realising that the horse might bolt again at the least thing, she, too, stopped.

'Kirstie?' Lisa called again.

'Give me a couple of minutes.' She waited until Cadillac had stopped striking his foot against the ground and had lowered his head; a signal that he was ready to be approached. Then she went slowly, smoothly, towards him, softly clicking her tongue and offering him the back of her hand to sniff at.

Only when he'd leaned forward to nudge at her hand with his soft grey muzzle did she reach out to take hold of the dangling halter rope.

'OK, got him!' she called to Lisa, breathing a sigh of relief.

Cadillac snorted. Through the mist Lucky whinnied back. Then both horses agreed to be led to the spot where the tent was pitched. Soon they were safely tethered once more.

'Lousy start to the day,' Lisa murmured, as Kirstie got busy with Lucky's tack.

Kirstie nodded. 'I wish I knew what spooked that bobcat.' Taking a saddle from the low branch of a nearby tree where they'd kept it overnight, she slung it over the palomino's broad back. Smoothly she brought the cinch strap under his belly and buckled it in place.

'I'll pack the tent.' More eager than ever to be out of there, Lisa slid the flexible rods out of their casings and collapsed the dome. Quickly she rolled up the lightweight fabric, only stopping to shake off the worst of the water drops. 'It's not that I let Matt's stuff about ghosts get to me,' she insisted. 'This place would've given me the creeps in any case. I mean, look at the horses; even *they* hate being here.'

'Looks that way.' Kirstie worked on, lost in thought, listening carefully to the sounds of streams full to the brim and rushing between rocks, over ledges. Water gushed and drowned out the other noises she might have heard: of the stealthy bobcat still circling the area, or maybe fox or coyote creeping through the undergrowth.

'So?' Lisa asked, when, a few minutes later, they were packed and mounted.

Kirstie took a deep breath, glancing up at the grey sky and round at the shadowy shapes of trees and hillocks. 'So I guess we should go down.'

'Down?' Lisa groaned. 'Into Dead Man's Canyon?'

She nodded. 'Something's down there, otherwise the bobcat wouldn't have acted the way he did. But you and Cadillac could stay here.' Kirstie glanced at the friendship-bracelet on her brown wrist; a gift from Lisa earlier that spring. She held her breath for the reply.

'No way. If you go, we go, don't we, Cadillac?'

Lisa read her mind. She held up her own matching bracelet.

'Not if you don't want to. Lucky and I can do this.'

In spite of everything, Lisa grinned. 'Liar, Kirstie Scott. You *need* me to come. You know you do!'

'OK, OK.' Kirstie realised that this was what was great about Lisa. She could be scared, but she would still go ahead and join in. 'Let's you and me cowboy up together!' she decided at last.

'There's even more water coming down here than yesterday!' Kirstie had dismounted now and was leading Lucky step by step down the track. Halfway along, she paused. It seemed that every ledge was now a waterfall and every jagged surface treacherously slippy.

'It's coming down from the high peaks,' Lisa pointed out. She and Cadillac had stopped a few paces behind. The mist clung to Lisa's dark red curls so that they stuck damply to her face. Wet from head to foot, her boots squelched water. 'You know, the storm hit pretty hard yesterday. That's why the streams are so full.'

'I guess.' Kirstie went on, letting Lucky pick the safest way. 'That's why, the more I think it through, I can't believe Glen Woodford when he said the stallion could've made it out of the canyon. Like, how, when there's all this water?'

Frowning, Lisa followed. 'You mean, it's hard enough when the ground's dry? But when it's wet, it's impossible?' She seemed to agree, then thought back to the previous day. 'But hey, how come there wasn't a single horse down there when we arrived?'

Kirstie stepped along a ledge where the water came up to the top of her boots. 'How do we know that?'

'We looked, remember! Zilch!'

'Only zilch from the ridge. I mean, how do we know for sure what we'll find when we get down?'

Lisa shivered, then pulled herself together. 'Yeah, like a whole bunch of wild horses were playing a game of hide-and-seek!'

Ignoring this, Kirstie led Lucky down a track she'd spotted which would take them all the way to the floor of the canyon. 'What we need is for this mist to clear,' she muttered.

But it still clung to the cliff and swirled into the crannies and crevices in the rocks. When they finally made it to ground level, it seemed thicker and damper than ever.

'So?' Lisa challenged again. Her voice was deadened by tall walls of rock which they could feel rather than see all around them. Stepping backwards, she blundered against a boulder and overbalanced into a deep, muddy puddle.

'Listen!' Kirstie let go of Lucky's rein, knowing that there was nowhere for him to bolt even if he had a mind to. The exit from the canyon was still blocked by the landslide, and the opposite end narrowed to a dead-end, as she knew. 'Did you hear something?'

'Yeah . . . water!' Lisa stepped out of the puddle and squelched anew.

'Right!' Kirstie reacted as if Lisa had really put her finger on something. 'Lots of water!'

'So what's new?' Except that her boots were full of the stuff. Dirty water was bubbling through the seams and out over the tops.

'I mean, like, *really* lots! A waterfall!' By now, Kirstie was convinced. She set off along the rock-strewn ground towards the narrow gulley at the top of the canyon. 'A new waterfall. Like, one where there wasn't one yesterday!'

'OK,' Lisa sighed. She took off her boots one at a time to shake out the muddy water. Then she ran to catch up. 'I believe you, but I still don't see . . .'

'Ssh!' Kirstie turned, finger to her lips, eyes wide. She'd reached the end of the canyon and come up against a sheet of water falling from a high ledge.

'Is this it?' Lisa craned her neck and stared up at the waterfall, created by several streams running together and meeting on the ledge some fifteen metres above the spot where they stood. It tumbled over fast and furious, splashing into a shallow pool at their feet.

Nodding, Kirstie walked up to the edge of the pool. She felt the spray on her face, noticed a lower ledge behind the fall which was almost dry because of a rocky overhang. 'Why isn't this pool deeper?' she queried, still listening, looking, investigating.

Lisa too studied the spot. It was clear that many gallons of water per second were pouring down the fall, but that the pool where it landed was neither big nor deep. 'Maybe the water drains out some place?'

Kirstie edged around the pool. 'But where? This is supposed to be the spot where Dead Man's Canyon ends. It's solid rock. There's no place for the water to run out.'

'Through here.' Lisa pointed to where the surface of the pool swirled with eddies and small currents. She saw that the water was channelled away at the base of the low ledge. 'There's a kind of stream at the back of the waterfall, beside this ledge.'

Quickly Kirstie ran to join her. 'Water can't run through solid rock!' she gasped. It could vanish underground, but what Lisa was saying was that it ran away in a stream above the ground. Which meant there was a gap in the rock!

'There's a gulley!' Lisa was still one step ahead. She was down on her hands and knees, crawling on to the ledge behind the fall.

Almost deafened by the crashing water, Kirstie followed. The ledge sloped downhill and ran the width of the waterfall.

'Hey!' Suddenly Lisa stopped.

'What? What is it?' All Kirstie could see was a sheet of water to her left, a wall of rock to her right, and Lisa in front.

'The stream runs along a kind of gulley.' Lisa turned to whisper, as if she could hardly believe what she saw. 'Like a chasm. Really narrow. But I think it opens out again.'

'Let's go!' Kirstie felt her stomach tighten into a knot. A hidden entrance to a place she never suspected before!

So they crept on, behind the thundering water, until the ledge flattened out, turned to the right and led them on between a narrow, tall crevice where the stream ran away from the waterfall.

'Hey,' Lisa whispered. 'Do we really want to do this?' She was squeezing down the gulley, up to her ankles in water, feeling closed in by tall rocks.

'We do,' Kirstie insisted. The gulley and the stream behind the fall held the answers to all her questions. She felt they would soon solve the mystery of the missing black stallion. 'We really do!'

* * *

There was a green clearing at the end of the hidden gap with the stream flowing gently across. Grass grew, aspen trees clung to the rocky slopes, dripping moisture. A well-kept, living secret behind Dead Man's Canyon.

'Did you know about this place?' Lisa stood in the small meadow shaking her head. She turned on the spot, looking all around.

Kirstie saw a pale brown hawk swoop from one of the trees, across the cloudy sky. 'No way!' she breathed.

A breeze swept through the grass. The aspen leaves quivered, the hawk landed.

'Does *anyone* know about it?' Lisa's voice didn't lift above a whisper.

'Charlie doesn't. I don't know if Hadley does. Maybe my grandpa did.' Kirstie stepped into the middle of the clearing. She noticed the bright blue columbines growing in the long grass. 'He'd know all the grazing land for the cattle. I used to come on round-ups in the spring and fall, but I never came here before.'

'. . . Kirstie!' Lisa broke in. She grabbed her arm and pointed.

There was a thicket of young aspens at the far side of the clearing. The trees were clustered thickly, good camouflage for any living creature.

Kirstie saw a dark movement. At first she thought it was a shadow cast by the trees. She looked again. The shape was solid. It moved silently between the slender trunks. Then it emerged.

The black stallion stood clear of the aspens. He raised his head, alert to their presence. He stayed calm, watching them, waiting.

'Oh, hey!' Lisa breathed. It was her first view of the magnificent horse.

'He's alive!' Kirstie closed her eyes. When she opened them, the stallion had taken a couple of steps towards them. 'And he's walking much better!'

They stared at his injured leg. There was no bandage around the knee. It was as Kirstie had guessed; her improvised strips of fabric had done the job of stemming the flow of blood, but soon afterwards, the horse must have torn them away with his teeth. In any case, the wound looked clean.

'You know something . . . ?' In turn, Kirstie took

a few steps towards the horse. 'The cut is starting to heal.'

'That's fast,' Lisa admitted.

'It's almost like . . . like . . .' She was peering hard across the clearing, not wanting to go too close and scare the stallion.

'. . . Like someone's put grease around it!' Lisa whispered.

'Antiseptic cream,' Kirstie agreed. Then she shook her head. 'No way!'

'Right. No way!' Lisa stared again and again at the injured knee. 'But there is *something* on that cut!' she insisted.

'How? . . . Who?'

Lisa screwed up her mouth and thought hard. 'Hadley?'

Kirstie shook her head. 'He'd have said.' By now she was sure; the stallion's right knee had been smeared with a thick coating of white grease.

'Glen Woodford?' Lisa guessed. 'Maybe he came back without telling us.'

'Nope.' Kirstie couldn't believe this either. 'In any case, that grease doesn't look like something a vet would use.' Glen would have relied on jabs of antibiotic and tetanus, and left the wound open, with maybe a stitch or two to hold it together. 'It looks more like a remedy an old rancher might have used.'

Lisa shook her head and sighed. 'OK,' she said. 'We have someone who sneaks into Dead Man's Canyon behind our backs, who gets close enough to this wild horse to lead him behind the waterfall into this clearing that no one else knows about . . .'

Keeping her eyes fixed on the wary horse, Kirstie nodded.

'. . . Who knows about old remedies and can get the stallion to trust him so he agrees to separate from the herd and stays here safe in the meadow . . .'

'Yep.' This needed plenty of thought. Kirstie knitted her brows and kept on staring.

'That takes one pretty smart guy!' Lisa looked round the green space. 'One smart, *invisible* guy!'

It was strange but true. The person who had helped the stallion must have been here either during those first hours after the landslide when Kirstie had gone with Charlie and Hadley to the ranch for help, or during the night, while Kirstie and Lisa had slept. He'd made no noise, but perhaps it was him who had spooked the bobcat early that morning. He'd treated the stallion, left him to graze in peace, and slipped away without leaving any clues.

'But who?' Lisa voiced the question.

Kirstie glanced away and up at the soaring hawk against the grey sky. She looked down again at the quiet, watchful stallion and felt the knot of worry she'd carried since they'd entered the gulley begin to ease.

'A healer,' she said quietly. 'An expert. Someone who really knows about horses.'

7

Matt threw another log on the ranch house fire, then quizzed Kirstie and Lisa. 'How come you're so sure the horse didn't find his own way into the clearing?'

Lisa stood with her back to the fire, her hands cupped around a mug of hot chocolate. She shook her head. 'No way would the stallion make it by himself. Anyhow, who cleaned up the wound and put the grease on?'

Kirstie's brother thought hard. 'So maybe Glen

Woodford went back to the canyon?'

'No, we already thought of that.'

'OK, so how about Smiley up at Timberline?' Matt was looking for answers that made sense.

Smiley Gilpin was a Forest Guard who lived at a station that stood at 10,000 feet. It was his job to look after the trails and plantations of ponderosa pines.

Lisa turned to Kirstie to see what she thought.

Staring into the flames of the fire in the huge grate, Kirstie shrugged. Right now the answers to the mystery didn't much interest her. Instead, she was enjoying the warmth, the feeling of relief that the black stallion was going to be OK. 'Give Smiley a call,' she suggested dreamily.

So Matt went off to the phone, leaving Lisa and Kirstie to relax. They'd arrived back at Half-Moon Ranch after their night on Miners' Ridge just after ten thirty, to find that Sandy Scott had already left with a group of beginners to ride Bear Hunt Trail. Charlie had taken the more advanced riders deep into the mountains, to Eden Lake. So the girls had dismounted in the empty corral, leaving Hadley to unsaddle Lucky and Cadillac. Then they'd come into the ranch house, to a barrage of questions from Matt.

'What do you think? Was it Smiley?' Lisa asked. She too was eager to solve the mystery of the unknown horse doctor.

Kirstie smiled and shrugged.

'I don't get it.' Lisa put her empty mug down on the stone hearth and sat cross-legged on the brown-and-white patterned rug. 'One minute you'd do anything for this horse: you sleep out, you have nightmares, you practically risk your neck. Now it's like you don't even care.'

Kirstie gazed at the fire as the burning logs shifted and sent up fresh sparks. 'I'm just glad, that's all.'

'But don't you want to know who's looking out for him?'

'Kind of.' She pictured a man, or maybe even a woman, who knew how to approach a wild horse and win his trust. Someone who cared enough to lead him behind the waterfall into the hidden clearing, where he would be safe. In a few days' time the stallion would be well enough to make his way back into the canyon and up on to Miners'

Ridge, when he would no doubt rejoin the rest of his herd.

As Lisa gave an exasperated shrug, Matt came back. 'Smiley says it ain't him,' he reported. 'The clearing behind the canyon is news to him.'

'Great,' Kirstie murmured absent-mindedly.

Matt frowned. 'What's great about it?'

'Don't ask!' Lisa warned. 'She's on a different planet. But how about Hadley? Maybe he could tell us more.'

'Let's ask,' Matt agreed briskly. He strode across the room, grabbing his stetson from the table.

Lisa sprang to her feet and dragged Kirstie after her. 'Hadley's been here forever,' she reminded them. 'We need to find out what he reckons.'

The old ranch hand was storing Lucky's saddle in the tack-room next to the corral when Matt, Lisa and Kirstie went to join him. They walked up the short ramp into the dark, cluttered room lined with iron hooks to hang bridles from and wooden racks for the saddles.

'Sure, I know the place,' he replied slowly after Matt had described the hidden clearing. 'Good grazing land.'

His answer, laid-back and matter-of-fact as usual, drew Kirstie into the conversation at last. 'You knew? How come you never told us about it?'

'You never asked.' Hadley hung Lucky's bridle alongside Cadillac's on the row of hooks.

'How can we ask about something when we don't even know it exists?' Kirstie pointed out. She'd known Hadley all her life, since the days when her grandparents had run Half-Moon Ranch as a cattle ranch. He'd always been the same; easygoing, unruffled, and sometimes infuriating.

The wrangler shrugged. 'Ain't had no call to go there since the spring of '94,' he told them. 'That was the last round-up me and your grandpa rode out on. We heard a bunch of cattle had found their way in there. And your grandpa knew every blade of grass round here. We had no problem tracking them down and rounding them up for the summer.'

'So other old ranchers would know the clearing?' Matt suggested after a short pause.

Hadley nodded. 'Jim Mullins over at Lazy B, Wes Logan up at Ponderosa Pines—'

'Maybe one of them helped the stallion,' Lisa cut in.

'Don't count on it,' Hadley warned, going to the door at the sound of horses returning along the trail by Five Mile Creek. 'Busy cattle men don't take time out to rescue a wild horse. More likely to be a backwoods man, I reckon.'

'A drifter?' Matt considered the new idea.

Kirstie had followed Hadley to the door. She took in her mother's group of riders returning slowly along the trail, gazed out at the Meltwater Range rising steeply from the narrow valley, then up at the sky. She saw that the clouds that had clung to the peaks for the past two days were clearing at last. There were small patches of blue, and more to come.

'One of those guys who live in trailers up there in the mountains?' Lisa prompted Hadley for more information. 'Kind of drop-outs?'

Kirstie knew the type of loner they were talking about. The backwoods men chose a lonely life of hunting and fishing. They scraped an existence from the land, lived simply, moved on.

'Like who?' Matt asked. 'Give us some names.'

Hadley tipped his hat back on his head. 'A name ain't much use without an address,' he reminded them. 'And these guys don't stay in one place too long.'

'But I know who you mean,' Lisa said eagerly. 'Some of them come into San Luis for supplies once in a while. They call in at mom's diner.' Her mother, Bonnie Goodman, ran the most popular eating place in town. 'Yeah, I got it; there's Bob Tyson. He's an ex-rodeo rider. Then there's Art Fischer and Baxter Black; hippy types. They all live kind of rough in the forest.'

Kirstie listened and let her imagination run on. She pictured the rescuer of the black stallion as a man who had turned his back on a life that centred on cars, jobs and evenings in front of the television. He knew the woods and the mountains, had learned the old ways; maybe even the habits and healing methods of the Native American Indians. One thing was for sure; the mystery man cared about horses.

'They live rough and think rough,' Hadley warned. He strode out into the corral to greet the returning riders, heading first for Ronnie Vernon on Silver Flash. He helped Vernon to dismount as he went on talking to Lisa. 'Don't go getting ideas about looking them up.'

'Ideas about looking who up?' Sandy Scott inquired as she dismounted from her own horse. She tethered the skewbald to the nearest post.

When she heard the news about the mysterious horse doctor and the latest theory on who he might be, she quickly agreed with Hadley. 'Too risky,' she told Lisa and Kirstie. 'We don't know the first thing about those guys.'

'Except that one of them cares enough about the black stallion to climb down into Dead Man's Canyon and take care of him!' Kirstie objected. 'Except that he's done more for that horse than a lot of people I can think of!'

'How do we know that?' Sandy took off her white hat, then linked arms with her daughter. She led her out of the corral, followed by Matt and Lisa. They walked together past the tack-room towards the ranch house. 'Aren't you loping ahead a little bit here?'

'But, Mom . . .' Kirstie launched into her reasons for tracking down the healer. 'He'd be real interesting. I reckon he knows a lot about wild horses. We could learn things from him . . .'

Sandy raised her eyebrows and stared. 'Too

risky,' she repeated. 'Hadley's right.'

'But . . .'

'Listen.' Her mother stopped on the stretch of grass outside the house, one foot on the wooden deck that led to the front door. She spoke seriously to get her point across. 'You paint a pretty picture of your horse doctor, but you gotta know that's not the way it's likely to be.'

'How come?' Matt asked. He saw that his mom meant what she said.

'Well, just suppose you've hit on the right answer and Bob Tyson, say, is the guy who's taking care of the stallion. Now I don't know Tyson in person, and I've never met him, but I hear he's got a bad name in town for not paying his bills.' Sandy turned to Lisa for confirmation.

'I guess,' Lisa agreed awkwardly.

'He lives real rough, he owes hundreds of dollars at the grocery store and the gas station and the diner. And one more thing I know about Bob Tyson . . .'

'What?' Kirstie suspected that she wasn't going to like this one little bit. Her stomach turned over and began to tie up in another knot.

'He does know plenty about horses, like you said. He used to work the rodeos in San Luis and Silvertown.' Sandy paused to fling her hat on to the porch swing, sat down, then delivered the bad news. 'So what he does now when he wants to scrape together a few dollars is go up the mountain and trail a herd of wild horses. He picks out the best horse in the bunch, watches and waits until he can cut that one out. Then he'll lasso it and bring it down. Great. Now he has something to sell at the horse sale.'

'What are you saying?' Kirstie gasped. She had a strong picture in her head of her own black stallion being brought down by a snaking lasso, of him being dragged into the dust, tied down, bullied until the fight went out of him. His gleaming black coat would be covered in dirt, there would be fear in his eyes.

'Bob Tyson catches wild horses to sell on to the rodeo circuit,' Sandy repeated. She looked long and hard at Kirstie, then Lisa, then Matt. 'So I'm telling all three of you right here; you don't tangle with the Bob Tysons of this world.'

'No, ma'am,' Lisa agreed and hung her head.

Matt gave a quick nod.

'Kirstie?' Sandy prompted.

She hung her head and gave in at last. 'OK,' she breathed, turning on her heel and striding away from the house.

8

So much for Kirstie's belief in her mysterious horse healer. She spent the rest of Sunday doing chores on the ranch, helping Matt and Charlie to bring in logs for the fires and stacking them outside the guest cabins, then raking the dirt surface of the arena behind the corral. That evening Charlie and Matt were to give an exhibition of horsemanship there, and everything must be made neat and tidy.

But Kirstie felt too let down to work well. It was like riding Lucky up to Hummingbird Rock, feeling great, seeing that the world was a beautiful place, then suddenly, unexpectedly, falling off. She was down on the ground, covered in dirt, looking like an idiot. And she only had herself to blame.

She raked the arena with sullen strokes, head down, eyes fixed on the furrowed pattern she made with the rake. Trust her to believe that the black stallion's helper was someone you could trust. All that stuff about knowing nature and caring about horses turned out to be Kirstie's own imagination running away with her, making up romantic stories that turned out not to be true.

'Sorry,' Lisa had said quietly after Sandy had dropped the bombshell. 'I know how much this means to you.'

Kirstie had done her best to smile back at her friend. 'Sure. But I guess we can still hope.'

'How come?' Lisa was waiting for her grandfather, Lennie Goodman, to drive over from Lone Elm, pick up her bicycle and drive her down to her home in San Luis. 'You heard what Hadley and your mom said. No way can we take any more risks to save the stallion.'

Inwardly Kirstie had groaned. But she didn't

show how disappointed she felt, and had waved Lisa off in her grandpa's red pick-up truck without giving anything away.

It was only when she was alone in the late afternoon sun, working in the arena, making it ready for the evening show that she admitted even to herself how bad it was.

For a start, she really loved and admired that horse. Her first view of him in the canyon, proud and suspicious, neck arched, nostrils flared as he protected his herd, had done it. Then there was his courage. She remembered how he'd struggled through his bewilderment and pain to get to his feet after the landslide. And the stallion had trusted her. Hers was the first human hand ever to touch him as she buckled the halter on to help him. And he'd believed in her as she strapped the bandage around his leg to stop the bleeding.

Fiercely Kirstie raked the ground. The horse had permitted her touch, had allowed her to help him. And now a second human being, a man whose name might be Bob Tyson, or Art Fischer, or Baxter Black, had deceived him. The mystery man had found him trapped in Dead Man's Canyon, had offered false help in order to make money out of him. The Drifter had betrayed the horse's precious trust for the sake of a few dollars in a San Luis sale barn.

Unless . . . unless . . . Kirstie stopped work and held the rake frozen in mid-air. 'How dumb am I?'

'You say something?' Charlie poked his head around the tack-room door. It was his afternoon to clean the tack while the others took rides along the trails. With his shirt sleeves rolled up, the low sun made him look extra-tanned.

'Yeah . . . Nope!' Quickly she worked over the last corner of the arena and flung the rake into one corner of the barn. Then she made sure Lucky was still hitched to his post in the corral before she went running into the tack-room to fetch his saddle.

Charlie stood to one side and watched. 'Looks like you changed your mind about riding this afternoon.'

'Yep.' She'd been so dumb. Sure, her mom had said to stay away from the backwoods men. And that made sense, if they were as tough as Sandy said they were. Kirstie had agreed that she wouldn't go riding up the mountain looking for their beaten-up old trailers, trying to convince them not to sell her beautiful wild stallion to some ruthless rodeo organiser.

That had been the exact promise: 'OK, I'll stay clear of Bob Tyson.'

'And Art Fischer, and Baxter Black, and any other drifter who happens to be passing through.' Sandy Scott had made the situation absolutely plain.

And, though it had felt as bad as teeth being pulled, Kirstie had promised.

But she *hadn't* promised her mom not to go back to Dead Man's Canyon.

'Can't say I blame you.' Unsuspecting, Charlie looked up at the blue sky and offered to help her saddle Lucky. 'I'd take a ride myself if I didn't have this exhibition tonight.'

'Tell Mom I'll be back before sundown.' Her fingers felt clumsy as she rushed to fasten the cinch and pull down the stirrups. She mounted quickly and took the reins.

'Sure thing.' Charlie stood and watched her set off, then called after her. 'Hey, your mom's gonna ask me where you went!'

Kirstie reined Lucky back. 'Tell her Meltwater Trail,' she yelled, turning again and riding off into the sun without looking back.

Meltwater Trail and Dead Man's Canyon. That was how dumb she'd been! It had taken her since lunch to realise that her promise to her mom didn't cover riding back to the hidden clearing, finding the stallion and setting him free.

Now it was all she could think about as she urged Lucky into a trot and then a smooth lope up the hill.

Again and again she went over each step of the new plan, almost forgetting to duck the branches of the pine trees and guide the palomino over fallen trunks as they sped on. The black stallion would still be there in his clearing behind the waterfall. Perhaps the rest of the herd would be gathered nearby. Kirstie would dismount and leave Lucky on the ridge. She would take a headcollar and rope with her, and climb down into the canyon. Then she would crawl along the ledge into the meadow. Then . . .

Kirstie lurched forward as Lucky came to a

sudden stop. They'd covered more ground than she'd realised and reached fast-flowing Horseshoe Creek. Now they would have to wade across before they reached the canyon. Lucky had been heading for his usual crossing place when a figure standing on a rock in the middle of the stream brought him to a halt.

It was a man with a fishing-rod and canvas bag slung across his shoulder, obviously making his way down towards Five Mile Creek in the valley below. Nothing about him looked unusual or scary; he was medium height, with fair, short hair, wearing a padded jacket, jeans and boots. But Sandy's recent warning was fresh in Kirstie's mind. What if this man, whom she'd never seen before, was one of the drifters they'd been talking about? Maybe he was Baxter or Art? Or maybe even the notorious Bob Tyson?

The thought made Kirstie rein Lucky to the right and head off across country without waiting to greet the stranger. She felt her horse begin to blow as the hill grew steeper and they passed under the shadow of Hummingbird Rock, but she pushed him on until they were out of sight.

Then she slowed. The detour was heading them towards Miners' Ridge; she recognised the weird humps of grassed-over mine waste on the horizon. Knowing that the ridge would give her a good view down into the canyon, and finding that Lucky had soon got his second wind, she decided to carry on.

They came on to the ridge as the sun began to turn the sky pink. The dark pines lined up in silhouette, tall and straight. And beneath the trees stood the horses.

'Easy!' Kirstie breathed. Lucky gently slowed and stopped. The breeze lifted her hair and cooled her hot face as they stood gazing at the herd.

They seemed like dream horses, still as statues under the trees. But the breeze reached them and swayed their long tails. One sorrel stamped and turned her head towards the onlookers, then turned to gaze again into the seemingly empty canyon.

How long had they been waiting there, Kirstie wondered. Maybe hours. While shadows lengthened and the light drained from the hillsides, they'd been watching. She noticed a dappled grey mare standing apart from the rest, nearer to the sheer drop into Dead Man's Canyon, her head forward, long ears pricked. The mare ignored Kirstie and Lucky, and gave a low snicker that rippled through the quiet air and was swallowed by the deep sides of the ravine.

The still, silent horses listened for a reply.

Kirstie shook her head. The mare had signalled to the black stallion below, but there had been no answer.

Restless now, the herd broke up and began to mill around. Two foals cut away from their mothers and skittered on long, ungainly legs towards a stream that ran into a gulley at a blocked entrance to an old mine. A young, strong blue roan stallion trotted a hundred metres along the ridge, and with a flick of his tail and a toss of his head, wheeled and came back.

But the grey mare hadn't given up. Standing at the brink, she gave another high whinny.

It sent a shiver down Kirstie's spine. The mare was demanding an answer from her injured mate.

And this time it came. A loud, piercing cry broke from the depths of the canyon, echoing against the rocks, rising to where the herd had gathered. The black stallion had given his reply.

Kirstie tied Lucky to a tree branch and climbed down the difficult but by now familiar route into the canyon. She carried a rope slung crossways across her shoulder, her mind fixed on carrying out her plan to set the stallion free.

But she knew she must be quick if she hoped to crawl along the ledge behind the waterfall and into the clearing, because the light was fading. There was time to do it if everything went well. But the stallion might prove difficult to catch and lead out. In that case, she would have to leave him there for one more night and come back early tomorrow.

What she hadn't expected was to find him still in pain from his injury. But when she stood upright after her wet crawl behind the waterfall and stepped on to the grass, and discovered the stallion standing at the furthest point beside the copse of young aspens, she saw that he couldn't yet take his weight on his left leg. The knee was bent, the hoof raised from the ground.

But maybe . . . Kirstie went slowly forward.

Maybe with her help he would be able to limp across the meadow, through the narrow chasm and along the ledge to freedom.

The stallion tossed his head and whinnied loudly. He shifted awkwardly, almost collapsing on to the left leg, then backing away.

Kirstie paused. The horse was more lame than she'd thought. The knee joint was swollen, the covering of white grease over the wound beginning to turn brown and dirty. He staggered again in an effort to keep her at a distance.

It was no good then. Her plan depended on him being well enough to follow her out of the clearing and up the difficult track on to the ridge. But it would have to wait. Kirstie sighed and turned away. Then she stopped. But what if The Drifter came back for the stallion before her? The Drifter – not The Healer, not The Mystery Horse Doctor, since Kirstie's talk with her mom – might force him out of the canyon, bad leg or not. He wouldn't care if the wild horse was in pain, not if he could make money out of him at the sale barn.

But what could she do? Nothing. Except keep watch. Kirstie took a deep breath and tilted her head to the darkening sky. One thing was for sure; no one in their right mind would come along after nightfall to move the stallion. They were safe at least until morning.

Encouraged, she made up her mind to leave the horse where he was.

'Until daylight,' she told him, as if he could understand. And in a way, he did.

Her gentle voice, her soft movements seemed to calm him. He no longer tried to back away, stumbling on his injured leg, but stood quite still. Head up, mane ruffled by a warm breeze that whispered through the aspens and up the steep cliffs on to the ridge above, he watched her go.

'I must be crazy,' Lisa complained. She yawned and slumped in the saddle. 'It's the first day of my vacation and I get up before dawn!'

Kirstie grinned. 'You know what we say at Half-Moon Ranch; you just gotta . . .'

'. . . Cowboy up!' Lisa groaned. 'Yeah, yeah.'

She'd driven out to the ranch with her mother in answer to Kirstie's secretive phone call of the night before. Kirstie had asked her to ride back to

Dead Man's Canyon with her to look out for the stallion, but she'd warned her not to say anything to her mom. As far as the adults were concerned, Lisa and Kirstie had simply organised a breakfast ride to celebrate the beginning of the school vacation.

The two women had been surprised that the girls wanted to ride out so early, but they'd shrugged, seen them off on Lucky and Cadillac and settled down to an early morning cup of coffee over the ranch-house kitchen table.

'Better to be crazy than mean,' Kirstie said now, thinking all the time of how they must beat The Drifter and his plan to sell the stallion.

'Huh.' Lisa piled on the groans. 'Just don't tell anyone I did this, OK?'

Her good-tempered complaints passed the time until Miners' Ridge came into view against a clear morning sky.

'Sun's gonna be hot today,' Kirstie predicted. 'It's gonna melt the snow off the peaks and send a whole lot more water down.'

As if to prove her point, Horseshoe Creek seemed even deeper and faster than it had the night before. Lucky went down the bank and stepped sturdily in, swaying slightly as the water rose round his flanks and soaked Kirstie's jeans. She urged him on and he surged through, then they turned to wait for a reluctant Cadillac.

'C-c-cold!' Lisa gasped, as she too felt the water dash against her legs.

But by the time the girls made it to the ridge the first rays of sun had dried off their jeans and they were both feeling good about the plan to take another look at the stallion.

'Even if his leg's not good enough to come out of the clearing with us, we'll try to get near and talk to him,' Kirstie said as she dismounted and tied Lucky up. 'The more he gets to know us, the easier it's gonna be in the long run.'

'We can always come back later today and try again if need be.' Lisa had been the first off her horse and was ready to take the track down into the canyon.

'Or stay out here the whole day and keep watch,' Kirstie said. She was on the lookout for the herd, expecting to see the grey mare at their head. The fact that they weren't here on the ridge surprised her slightly.

'You can't be serious!' Lisa retorted, thinking of her stomach as usual. 'Stay here the whole day without a sack-lunch?'

She went on ahead, grumbling and kidding, but Kirstie stayed on the ridge, still looking out for the wild horses. She thought she heard the faint sound of hooves drumming down the hillside towards her, and then she caught sight of the young sorrel, quickly followed by a piebald. They galloped through the trees, kicking up dirt, swerving past boulders. 'Hey!' she said softly. These horses weren't playing a game of chase. Their flattened ears and reckless speed told her they were fleeing from an unseen pursuer.

Two young foals came next, skidding down the slope, their stick-like legs folding under them as they crashed down. They jerked back up on to their feet and ran on. Then more fully-grown horses came hard on their heels. Kirstie saw the fear running through their bodies, making them toss their heads and rear up. What was it? Who was chasing them?

'Say, what's happening?' Lisa had heard the noise and climbed back on to the ridge. She stopped and stared.

Kirstie took a step forward, then another. Here came the grey mare at the back of the herd, half-hidden by a cloud of dust. The horse ran more slowly, hindered by something that she couldn't quite make out.

'What's that around her neck?' Lisa cried. 'See; she's dragging a length of rope!'

Kirstie broke into a run. She saw it now; the rough slip-knot, the trailing rope that caught in the bushes as the horse ran.

The other wild horses had reached the ridge and galloped along its length. But the grey mare was winded. She saw the girls, slowed and wheeled away. Up on her hind legs, front hooves flailing, she whirled back the way she'd come.

But her path was blocked. There was a man scrambling down the mountain towards her; a dark figure in a black hat, the brim pulled well down. He spread his arms wide to threaten the mare, paused to unhitch another rope from his shoulder, then raised it over his head to launch a second lasso.

124

'Don't do that!' Kirstie yelled the first words that came into her head. She ran faster, straight at the grey horse.

Caught between them, the mare reared up.

The second rope snaked through the air. Kirstie leaped forward, jumped and caught it. The man's harsh voice swore. He jerked at the rope and heaved Kirstie off her feet.

'Let go of the damn rope!' he cried.

She hung on. Her arms felt as if they were being pulled out of their sockets as the stranger dragged her over the rough ground.

'Get out of my way!' he yelled again. 'I plan to rope that mare in, and no fool kid's gonna stop me!'

9

'Kirstie, let go of the rope!' Lisa begged.

Kirstie was cut and bruised, covered in dirt. But she'd hung on long enough to give the grey horse a chance to get away. Out of the corner of her eye she saw the mare turn on the spot and race along the ridge after the other wild horses. Her white mane and tail streamed in the wind. OK; *now* Kirstie would loosen her grip!

'Damn fool kid!' the man shouted, falling back as the tension on the rope suddenly slackened. He jerked it and began to coil it towards him.

Quickly Lisa helped Kirstie to her feet. She pointed at the scratches on her arms. 'You're bleeding!'

'I'm OK.' Breathing hard, her shoulders and hands hurting, she brushed herself down. 'No way was I gonna stand by and watch that!'

'But listen!' Lisa was pulling her urgently away from the angry man. 'You know who that is? It's Bob Tyson!'

Kirstie sniffed then breathed out rapidly, as if she'd been punched in the stomach. 'You sure?'

Lisa nodded. 'I've seen him in the diner.'

Glancing across, Kirstie took in the frowning features under the wide brim of the black hat. The man was unshaven and thickset, wearing a dark grey shirt and old jeans. The large silver buckle of his belt glinted in the light as he finished coiling his lasso and strode towards them.

'I could have roped that horse in if you hadn't gotten in the way!' he snarled at Kirstie. 'You know how long I'd been on her tail? Since sun-up. I had her real tired and cut off from the herd. And you had to mess-up!'

Kirstie drew herself up, tall as she could. Her

grey eyes flashed as she spoke. 'I'm glad.'

'Me too.' Lisa stood alongside. Together they could defy the horse rustler.

'No way does that mare belong in a sale barn!' Kirstie went on angrily. 'Her place is here on the mountain. This is where she belongs.'

'Along with the stallion,' Lisa added. She glared at Tyson to let him know they knew what he was up to.

But the man's face switched at the mention of another horse. His eyes narrowed, he became suspicious. 'Stallion?' he repeated.

'Quit pretending you don't know what I'm saying,' Lisa raced on. 'One black stallion in one hidden clearing!'

Kirstie watched Tyson's frown deepen. His eyes flicked shrewdly from Lisa to herself and back again.

'Oh, *that* black stallion,' he sneered.

'The one you're gonna take to the sale barn when his leg's good!' Lisa challenged. 'Only you'd better know, we're not gonna let you!'

'Shh!' Kirstie snatched at her friend's arm and began to pull her away. 'Let's get out of here!'

'I'm gonna take a stallion to the sale barn

when his leg's good?' Tyson echoed. He glanced thoughtfully up and down the hillside, then along Miners' Ridge. His gaze rested on the cliff edge and the steep drop into Dead Man's Canyon. 'A stallion in a hidden clearing?'

'Let's go!' Kirstie insisted.

'Quit pulling me!' Lisa protested. But she gave in when she saw the look of panic on Kirstie's face. She glanced again at Tyson's sneering features with a dawning realisation of what she'd done.

They left the drifter standing on the ridge, grinning after them. Running for their horses, they mounted and rode away. Away from the old mine entrance and the grassy mounds, away from the stream swollen by meltwater from Eagle's Peak. Away from Dead Man's Canyon and the horse in the hidden clearing.

'He didn't know!' Kirstie gasped at Lisa as they found the trail and pushed Lucky and Cadillac on in any direction as long as it was away from the horse rustler. 'I was watching his face all the time you stood up to him, and it hit me right between the eyes. That was the first Tyson ever heard of the black stallion!'

* * *

And now Lisa and Kirstie had to pray that the drifter didn't know the mountain well enough to discover the clearing behind the waterfall.

'After all, even the Forest Guard doesn't know about it,' Kirstie reminded her friend as they reached level ground and carried on along Five Mile Creek Trail. They tried to convince themselves that Tyson had no chance of finding the stallion. 'And no more does Charlie, and he's been riding these trails with the intermediates since winter.'

'Whereas this guy's a loner, a drifter. He moves on before he gets to know a place real well.' Lisa nodded hard. 'He shoots a few deer, catches a few fish . . .'

'Builds up a whole pile of debts . . .' Kirstie added.

'Sells a few horses that don't belong to him . . .'

'Until the sheriff rides him out of town.' She wished she felt as confident as they both sounded. She wished her heart would stop thumping and jumping with fear every time she pictured Tyson. Most of all, she wished she could think of a plan to deal with the new emergency.

'I don't reckon he'll ever find the way into the clearing!' Lisa insisted. 'My guess is, he'll forget what we told him about the stallion and keep on after the grey mare.'

'I guess.' Kirstie sighed. 'But you gotta admit, we've been wrong about a whole lot of things . . .' She tailed off, realising that they'd jumped to too many conclusions since yesterday, when they'd seized on the idea that it was a drifter up to no good who'd hidden the injured stallion in the clearing.

'You're right.' Lisa's face fell. 'We can't rely on Tyson not finding the stallion.'

They were silent for a while, as they rounded a bend in the creek and the scattered, single-storey log buildings of Half-Moon Ranch appeared in the distance.

'What we have to do is beat Tyson at his own game,' Kirstie decided. 'Now he knows about the horse, he's gonna find him for sure. Sooner or later.'

'Let's hope it's later.' Lisa gave Cadillac his head and let him trot for home.

Lucky too gained speed. 'So what we do is go back and get the horse out of there before Tyson shows up!' Kirstie insisted. 'Only this time, we get your grandpa to come along with his earth-moving machine.'

'Which he plans to do in any case.' Lisa told her that he'd mentioned it again on the drive to Half-Moon Ranch that morning. 'He knows he's still gotta move that heap of rocks and clear the entrance to the canyon,' she confirmed.

Encouraged, Kirstie went on. 'He bulldozes a way through the landslide while we fetch the horse from the clearing. Sure, the stallion can't climb up the cliff because of his bad leg, but walking right out of there on a level track once your grandpa's finished work; that's different. I reckon he could do that easy.'

Lisa nodded. 'It sounds a pretty good plan . . . if Grandpa agrees. And your mom too.'

If . . . if. If they beat Tyson to it. If the bulldozer could be brought across to Dead Man's Canyon in time. Urging their horses into a lope along the final stretch of flat ground, Kirstie and Lisa raced for the ranch.

* * *

'What I don't get is, if Tyson ain't the guy who's been looking after the stallion in the clearing, then who the heck is?' Matt spoke what was in everyone's thoughts. It was the one thing that still puzzled him, even as he rode out with Lisa and Kirstie, back to Miners' Ridge.

The girls had done a good job of convincing everyone that they needed to act fast if they were to save the black horse. Sandy Scott had returned from her morning ride and listened intently as they described the new developments, including the sighting of Tyson. She'd immediately called Lennie Goodman, who had agreed to drive the earth-mover straight over from the trailer park to the canyon. He'd estimated that it would take him a couple of hours to get there in the slow, heavy vehicle.

Matt had promised Sandy that he wouldn't let Kirstie and Lisa out of his sight all afternoon, and she'd finally reluctantly agreed to let them return to the ridge.

'Watch and wait until Lennie's bulldozed a way in,' she'd insisted. 'Then go get the stallion and lead him right out.'

Kirstie had stood at the kitchen door, shifting guiltily from one foot to the other. 'Got it,' she muttered.

'And don't even *think* of doing anything except that.' Her mom had been deadly serious. 'Straight into the clearing, straight out again. If his leg's strong enough, let the stallion go. No fooling around bringing him back to the ranch to keep an eye on him.'

'No way!' Kirstie had protested.

'You gotta be tough.'

'Sure.' She'd turned and crossed the deck, taken the two steps down on to the grass and run for the corral ahead of Lisa and Matt. She could dream of caring for the beautiful black horse, of brushing him until he gleamed, of giving him the best feed and watching his every move. But that would mean surrounding him with fences, penning him in. No, that would never work. The stallion needed freedom.

By the time she, Lisa and Matt were heading for the canyon, she'd squashed her dream and faced reality.

135

* * *

It was mid-afternoon by the time the three riders reached Miners' Ridge. The sun had scorched away the last of the clouds and now shone down from a deep blue sky. Yet more meltwater from the ice-bound peaks swelled the streams. In the distance, they heard the slow rumble of Lennie Goodman's bulldozer as it made its way along a lower trail.

'Remember, we stick together,' Matt reminded Kirstie and Lisa, picking up the girls' impatience as they reined their horses in by the cave-like entrance to the old mine. Since Lisa was riding Cadillac, he'd picked out Crazy Horse for himself; a big, ugly-beautiful pale tan horse with white socks and fair mane and tail.

Kirstie dismounted, then stared down into Dead Man's Canyon for signs of Bob Tyson's presence, but all seemed quiet. 'How about we all go down to check?'

The others agreed that there could be no harm in climbing into the canyon and making sure that the stallion was still safe in the clearing.

'Let's take the horses,' Lisa suggested. 'If Tyson's still hanging around the area, he could spot them, guess what we plan to do and beat us to it.'

Matt nodded. 'You and Lucky lead the way,' he told Kirstie.

So she went ahead on foot, leading the palomino, keeping a watch for any unusual movement or sound from below.

'Did you hear that? Like, branches moving, twigs snapping!' Lisa hissed. She and Cadillac were halfway down the track into the canyon, hard on Kirstie's heels, but she stopped dead and glanced anxiously back up at the ridge. 'I got this weird feeling someone's watching us!'

Third in line with Crazy Horse, Matt scanned the jagged overhangs. The heat of the sun made steam rise from the dark red rocks. He shook his head.

'Yes, I kind of . . . feel it!' Lisa protested. 'Like eyes are on us all the time!'

'Those miners' ghosts keep showing up.' Matt shrugged off the uneasy feeling that Lisa had created.

But Kirstie took her friend more seriously. She watched out for movement, saw sinister shapes in shadows, could almost pick out Tyson's dark hat and crouching figure. But no; when she looked hard, there was no one there. 'Come on!' she whispered. 'Let's go see the stallion!'

Pushing ahead, wading with Lucky through a new stream that came gushing over the ridge and across their path, Kirstie was suddenly overtaken by a fresh rush of anxiety. Not concentrating, the force of the clear, cold meltwater almost knocked her off her feet and made her lurch to catch hold of Lucky's saddle horn. Her horse stood steady long enough for her to pull herself upright and wade to safety.

'You OK?' Matt shouted above the sound of splashing water.

'Yep.' More determined than ever, she pressed on.

'When you get to the bottom, wait there for us!' her brother yelled.

Kirstie glanced back to see that Lisa was also having trouble crossing the stream. Matt seemed to be telling her to mount Cadillac and try riding across. But the ledge where they all stood was narrow, and the hold-up lengthened. Meanwhile, Kirstie decided to continue.

So much meltwater. Water everywhere. It dripped off every ledge, trickled into narrow streams. The small streams joined together to form wide waterfalls that bounced and crashed off the rocks all around.

But, while Lisa struggled with Cadillac halfway down the cliff, Kirstie and Lucky made it to the bottom. She looked back up to see where they'd come, and in a way she was relieved to see how difficult the route had been. Surely Bob Tyson would have found it impossible to pick out the way. Which meant that, most important of all, the stallion was still safe . . .

Impatiently Kirstie glanced at the main waterfall that hid the ledge entrance to the clearing. She frowned at the torrent of water that crashed into the pool at the foot of the fall. Surely the pool hadn't been that deep before? And surely the waterfall hadn't completely hidden the ledge!

Suddenly she realised what was happening. The floodwater from the melting mountain glaciers, combined with the rain from the weekend storms, would soon make it impossible to use the entrance. The water would rise faster and faster as the sun continued to melt the snow, and soon it would cut them off from the clearing!

There was no time to lose. Swiftly Kirstie ran to the edge of the pool. Obviously, the narrow channel between the rocks behind the waterfall had been blocked by driftwood and other debris, so the floodwater couldn't drain away into the stream that flowed across the clearing. Instead, it was rising rapidly over the ledge.

Telling Lucky to stay where he was, she waved both arms and yelled up at the figures on the cliff. 'Matt, Lisa; I'm going ahead into the clearing!'

Matt's reply was drowned by the sound of the waterfall. In any case, it made no difference. Nothing would stop her from checking on the black horse.

Kirstie stumbled and splashed through the pool, taking a short cut towards the vanishing ledge. Already soaked through, she hauled herself up and began to crawl behind the thundering fall. The water splashed white and foaming all around. Dark rock towered to one side; to the other was a wall of water.

She gasped and crawled on down the sloping

ledge. Water was tumbling on to her, bowing her under its force. She had to close her eyes, hold her breath, crawl on, until at last she reached the end of the ledge. Now she could squeeze into the narrow, water-filled gap between two rock-faces. She could fumble with her fingertips along the stone corridor, feeling the water hammering down on to her, resisting the rush of the stream as it tried to sweep her along.

But, before the end of the gulley, she found an obstacle blocking her way. It was as she thought; a heavy log had jammed across the gap, and a pile of stones and brushwood had collected against it. Water was building up behind the jam, which Kirstie would have to climb to get into the clearing. Steadying herself, feeling the current swirl around her legs and up to her waist, she dragged herself over the sodden barricade.

On the far side she eased herself down into the clearing. She pushed the wet hair from her face and took a deep breath. After the roar and crash of the waterfall came the peace and quiet, the green trees and grass, the black horse in the sunlight.

He stood by the stream as if waiting, his left leg

raised from the ground, head up, ears turned towards her.

So beautiful. Caught up in the spell of his powerful presence, Kirstie walked towards him. To her amazement and delight, the horse responded by stepping forwards; one, two, three paces. His injured left leg took his weight, his limp was much less than before. Kirstie smiled at the sight of the stallion's steady approach.

But only a few metres behind her, the flood-water was rising. She glanced back. The strong current pressed at the log jam, shifting stones, trickling through the gaps into the already swollen stream.

Then suddenly, as she was about to turn to the stallion and reassure him, the main log gave way. Kirstie heard the dam burst and the water rush through in a torrent. With a gasp she prepared to stand her ground.

The powerful wave roared at her and engulfed her, knocked her off her feet, swept her on. She went under, flung out her arms, tried to grab at something solid as the current twisted and turned her. She came up, dragged air into her lungs, sought to save herself.

The stallion was her only hope. He stood in the path of the surging stream. Water swirled around his legs, his chest. It swept Kirstie directly towards him. She closed her outstretched arms around his neck, felt him lose his footing and slide into the water with her.

Then he was floating. She was clinging to his neck, the horse's magnificent head was clear of the water and he was swimming through the flood, carrying her to safety.

10

The stallion's strength lifted Kirstie clear of danger. She clung to him, clutching at his mane until his feet found solid ground. The water tugged at her, testing her grasp, but she held fast, felt the horse stand firm, then managed to straddle his back as he stepped out of the raging flood.

When he reached dry land, she found herself slumped forward, her head against his wet black mane, her arms still circling his powerful neck.

Kirstie breathed out with a sob and a groan. In

the instant when the cold floodwater had closed over her head, she'd faced death. A moment's noisy confusion, then clarity and silence, before she'd put her arms around the horse and been saved.

'That was a pretty neat piece of luck,' a voice said.

She looked up and all around. The voice had belonged to a stranger, not to Matt or Lisa or Lennie Goodman. Bob Tyson then? She tried to match The Drifter's low, mean tones with the voice she'd just heard.

'You could say that horse just saved your life.'

A figure was walking towards her as she slid quietly from the stallion's back. She could see a man's legs as she crouched beside the horse; legs in jeans and cowboy boots.

'I guess that evens things up. You dig him out from under a heap of rocks. He saves you from drowning.' The voice was light, even amused. The booted feet came to a halt a few metres from them. 'Kinda neat, like I said.'

Kirstie stood up and stepped to one side of the stallion. She shivered and dripped as she came face to face with the one witness to the stallion's courage.

'Art Fischer.' The man held out a hand for her to shake. 'I would'a helped too, only I was too far off.'

She stared at the hand, then the checkered padded jacket. She looked up at a pair of brown eyes in a smiling face; smiling as if she hadn't nearly drowned back there.

'You saw me yesterday by Hummingbird Rock,' he reminded her. 'Horseshoe Creek, remember?'

The man with the fishing-rod! 'Yep.' She nodded hard, sensing the black horse turn away from her and towards the man. 'We thought you were Bob Tyson . . . that is, Lisa . . . she heard a noise . . . were you watching us?'

It was the man's turn to nod. The smile seemed to stay on his face, around his eyes, even though it had faded from his lips. 'Tyson moved on,' he told Kirstie.

'When?' The news was slow to sink in through the questions flying round inside her head.

'Midday. He gave up on the grey mare he wanted once the Forest Guards got on his case. Didn't stop

146

to say too many goodbyes before he packed up his trailer and left.' Art Fischer watched and waited for the horse to leave Kirstie's side. He studied the injured leg as he limped slowly towards him.

'You told Smiley Gilpin?' Kirstie frowned. Slowly she puzzled out what had happened.

Art gave another slight nod. Gently he greeted the stallion by rubbing his long nose with the back of his hand.

'He lets you get pretty friendly, doesn't he?' She noticed that the stallion had no fear around Art.

'I guess.'

'You wouldn't say he was a wild horse to look ... at ... him now ...' Kirstie slowed down and tailed off. The stallion nuzzled Art's hand, then pushed at his chest with his dark muzzle. 'How come?'

Letting her work out the answer for herself, Art scratched the stallion's forehead and ran an expert hand along the animal's neck and across his shoulder. Then he stooped to examine the injured knee.

Kirstie watched the man inspect the wound to check that the swelling was down and the horse was able to bend the joint. She saw him reach into his jacket pocket and take out a tub of white cream. He unscrewed the lid, dipped in his fingertips and gently began to smear ointment on to the jagged cut.

'Art is the mystery healer!' Kirstie told Lisa.

Together she and the quiet stranger had made their way along the ledge behind the waterfall into Dead Man's Canyon.

Lisa stared as if she was seeing a ghost. 'We never thought you'd make it out of there!'

'Well, I did, thanks to the stallion. And listen, Art's the one who led him into the clearing first of all; not Bob Tyson!' Kirstie was dripping wet and shaking all over. 'Art's been taking care of him ever since the landslide. Isn't that great?'

Matt stepped forward to sling his jacket around her shoulders. 'Save it for later,' he said quietly. He squeezed her gently and kept one arm around her while she went on regardless.

'Tyson wasn't the only one who knows all the old stuff about horses. Art here picked it up from his grandpa when he was a little kid. His folks had a ranch over by Aspen Falls before they built the Interstate highway there. Then they moved away to Colorado Springs, but Art didn't like the city. He lives in a trailer up at Eden Lake. That's where he first saw the wild horses . . .'

'Whoa!' Art Fischer stopped staring at his wet boots, looked up and spoke for the first time. 'I didn't reckon on you telling them my whole life story.'

'But it's brilliant! You taught yourself the medicine stuff by working alongside your grandpa. And you've remembered all of it!' Art had explained everything in answer to her breathless questions in the clearing. Then, once he was satisfied that the unexpected swim hadn't done the horse too much harm, they'd left him in peace and quickly come back to the canyon.

'I guess. But no way do I want folks knocking on my door pestering me with damn fool questions,' he protested. 'I got a quiet life up by the lake, and that's the way I like it.'

Kirstie bit her lip and blushed. 'You're not mad at me?' To her, Art was her new hero. He might not look or sound like one, with his faded clothes, his shy way of hanging his head and his quiet, funny voice, but what he'd done for the black stallion made him number one in her eyes.

He smiled now and shook his head.

But, as if in answer to Art's fears that his privacy was about to be invaded, the sound of Lennie Goodman's bulldozer rumbling up Meltwater Trail broke the silence of the mountain. And up on the ridge, a group of trail-riders appeared with Hadley at their head. The line strung out along the cliff edge, staring down at the small group standing in the canyon.

'Hey, Art!' Hadley stood up in his stirrups and hollered. 'How are y'all?'

'Hey!' Art answered. He turned his head away from the onlookers, ducked his head and shrugged.

Kirstie stared from one to the other; the old wrangler on the ridge riding Yukon, her new friend standing by her side. 'You know him?' Cupping her hands to her mouth, she yelled up at Hadley.

'Sure I know him. He's Fenney Fischer's boy from Aspen Falls.'

'How come you didn't tell us?' she cried.

And back came the slow, inevitable answer, as Hadley led the riders on along the ridge: 'How come you never asked?'

'I got a real nice site at Lone Elm,' Lennie told Art later that same evening. The bulldozer had shifted tons of rock and earth, and the entrance to Dead Man's Canyon was clear at last. 'It's got running water, I can connect you up to the electricity generator, no problem.'

Art listened and smiled.

Lisa's grandpa described the advantages of moving down from lonely Eden Lake to the comforts of an official trailer park. 'Hot showers, a grocery store right on site, folks to get along with on a long winter's night.'

Kirstie raised her eyebrows at Lisa, slipped an arm through hers and wandered away from the group. She was happy that the blocked entrance had been cleared, glad that Matt had contacted their mom on the radio and that Sandy and Hadley had made it to the canyon with a set of dry clothes for Kirstie and in time to see Lennie's giant machine complete the job.

Now it was evening. The sun was setting, shadows creeping down the silent mountain.

'What do you reckon? Will Art take Grandpa's vacant site?' Lisa asked as they strolled towards the waterfall.

'Nope.' Kirstie grinned. 'Folks can come knocking too easy with their damn fool questions in a trailer park.'

Lisa glanced back at Art, standing now a little way apart from Matt and Sandy Scott, her grandpa and Hadley. 'He's kinda shy.'

'Kinda.' She took a deep breath and gazed up at the sparkling, rushing water. Beyond the fall, beyond Miners' Ridge and way past Eagle's Peak in the far distance, the sun was disappearing from the sky. 'He says dawn tomorrow we can let the stallion go free,' she told Lisa softly. 'Do you want to be here?'

Tuesday sunrise. Before the guests at Half-Moon Ranch were stirring, while Matt and Sandy, Hadley and Charlie were bringing in the horses from the ramuda, brushing them down and saddling them up for the day's rides, Kirstie rode out with Lisa to Dead Man's Canyon.

Though the sun was just up and the air still sharp with an overnight frost, Art Fischer was there before them.

'Hey,' he said quietly.

'Hey, Art.' The girls dismounted and tied up Lucky and Cadillac.

Then they all three went along the ledge behind the fall to bring the black stallion out of the clearing.

He was grazing by the young aspen trees. When he saw them, he came quietly, curiously, taking his weight nicely on the left front leg, the limp almost gone. Kirstie and Lisa held their breaths, and as he came close, they gazed up into his deep brown eyes.

He scarcely noticed when Art quietly slipped a halter rope around his neck. It tightened. He pulled away once, then accepted it.

Art spoke gently to him, rubbing the back of his hand up and down his long face. 'Easy, boy. Time for you to leave this place.'

The horse heard and followed the man along the

bed of the stream, out of the clearing between the tall rocks of the dark gulley. Not even the narrow ledge behind the waterfall spooked him. He just went straight along it, right after Art Fischer.

Lisa and Kirstie watched with silent awe the trust between horse and man.

'It's magic!' Lisa breathed as they came out into the canyon and saw Art prepare to release the stallion.

He turned to Kirstie. 'Say goodbye?'

She nodded and went forward, feeling tears prick her eyelids. A happy-sad goodbye. A good goodbye to a horse whose life she'd helped to save – and who had helped to save hers too. She reached out with a trembling hand to stroke his lovely face.

The stallion bowed his head.

Then Art led him towards the cleared exit. He loosened the halter rope and slipped it off.

'Bye,' Lisa whispered.

Kirstie stood silent.

Then Art tapped the horse's shoulder with the flat of his hand. He clicked with his tongue.

The stallion stepped forward, hesitated, looked back at them.

From up above, high on Miners' Ridge, a horse whinnied. It was the grey mare, standing in the morning sun, her white mane bright. Behind her, in the shadows of the ponderosa pines, the wild herd waited.

The black horse looked up. He pawed the earth with one front hoof, stretched out his magnificent head and called back.

Then he reared and whirled. He was gone; out through the narrow gap cleared by the machine, up on to the trail that led to the ridge. He loped

with the wind in his black mane and tail, dark against the red rocks, the tall green trees; like a shadow, like a dream . . .

He was gone.

RODEO ROCKY

JENNY OLDFIELD

Illustrated by
Paul Hunt

a division of Hodder Headline Limited

Rodeo Rocky

With thanks to Bob, Karen and Katie Foster, and to the staff and guests at Lost Valley Ranch, Deckers, Colorado

First published as a single volume in Great Britain in 1999
by Hodder Children's Books

1

'... Yup, I guess over the years I broke just about every bone in my body,' Hadley Crane told Kirstie Scott.

The head wrangler at Half-Moon Ranch leaned on the fence at San Luis Competition Grounds to reminisce. His white stetson was pulled well forward to shield his lined, brown face, his grey eyes were alert to the activity in the arena.

Kirstie too watched the team-roping competition with mounting interest. The next steer was made ready, prodded and pushed into the narrow wooden

1

chute. Two riders entered chutes to either side. They sat astride tough, well-built quarter horses – horses that had been trained to round up cattle on the ranches that nestled in the foothills of the Colorado Rockies. The nerves of both riders and horses were strung tight as the steer barged and kicked inside its narrow trap, demanding to be released into the arena.

'I broke my left leg three times,' Hadley went on. 'My hip got trampled, I dislocated this right shoulder more times than I can count . . .'

'All in rodeo accidents?' Kirstie stood on the bottom bar of the white fence to get a better view. The barrier went up, the steer charged into the dusty ring.

'Sure thing. Mostly bulldogging; that's a mighty risky event, when you have to land on eight hundred pounds of bullock and wrestle him down. And bronco riding; that's bad too.' Hadley watched the red steer raise the dust as it skidded to a halt across the arena, turned right around and charged back the way it had come.

After a ten second delay, the two cowboys were let loose too. Whooping and yelling, digging their spurs deep into the horses' flanks and with the cries of a sizeable San Luis crowd in their ears, they swung their ropes and headed for the bullock.

Kirstie winced as the first rope circled the bullock's head and the noose tightened. The frightened animal was dragged to a sudden halt. Now it kicked and writhed as the second cowboy swung his lasso. She glanced up and read the bold words printed on the banner that fluttered in the breeze over the entrance to the arena: 'Keeping the Dream Alive!'

'I always feel sorry for the steers,' she told Hadley quietly.

The ex-rodeo man shrugged and smiled briefly. 'Yup. But I reckon you're soft on *any* critter with four legs. Seems to me, you like 'em better than the two-legged kind.'

Kirstie didn't deny it. She watched the second cowboy, the heeler, lasso the steer's back legs and jerk him to the ground. The poor animal lay bound and helpless in the dust as the horses pranced and the riders dismounted.

'Nine point six seconds!' the voice on the loud-speaker announced. The crowd of two thousand people roared and cheered.

Quickly they untied the defeated animal and

3

cleared the arena, ready for the next team. Scores flashed up on the electric scoreboard.

'Hey, Kirstie.' Lisa Goodman sidled up to her friend to watch the closing stages of the competition. She wrinkled her nose at the grey dust that blew out of the arena, then brushed her white sweatshirt and ran a hand through her curly red hair.

'Hey,' Kirstie replied, eyes narrowed and fixed on the next steer lined up in the chute.

'Tell me never to wear white to the rodeo,' Lisa grumbled, squinting down at her grubby sweatshirt.

'Never wear white . . .' Kirstie began.

Lisa jostled her sideways. 'Not now – next time!'

'*What* next time?' As Kirstie turned to glance at her best friend, the wind blew her fair hair in wisps across her hot face. There was grit in her eyes and a growing sensation that this would be her last visit to the competition grounds. 'Tell me never to come to another rodeo again,' she countered.

'OK: never come . . .' Lisa's voice was drowned by the cheers of the crowd as the final bullock was released.

'Isn't this great?'

'Wow, did you see that last team? Nine point

two seconds to rope that bullock!'

'It came out of the squeeze like a black bullet! Those guys sure knew how to rope a steer!'

Eager voices commented on the team-roping event as the crowd waited for the result.

'OK, Kirstie?' Sandy Scott joined her daughter, Lisa and Hadley at the ringside. A taller, older version of Kirstie, with the same fair hair and large, grey eyes, she wore a pale straw stetson and light denim shirt over her blue jeans and tan cowboy boots, and was followed by a bunch of guests from Half-Moon Ranch.

'Hmm.' Kirstie chewed her lip and said nothing, knowing that the rodeo wasn't her mom's favourite thing either. It was the ranch guests whose eyes had lit up when they heard about the regular San Luis event. They'd asked Sandy to drive them the fifteen miles into town, so they could cheer, clap, take photographs and enjoy the hustle and bustle of the July show day.

'What's next?' one hyped-up kid asked Hadley. The dark-haired, eleven-year-old boy climbed up on the fence and sat kicking his heels against the wooden rails. He looked eagerly across the arena towards the empty chutes.

5

'Wild horse race,' the wrangler mumbled, low and slow. 'You have teams of three men trying to get a saddle on a wild mustang and ride him round that track, see?' He pointed towards a race course that ran for half a mile around the perimeter of the competition grounds. ''Course, the mustang don't wanna know. He was out on the plains of Wyoming a couple of days back, before they drove a truck out there to rope him in and drive him here specially for the competition.'

'Cool!' Brett, the young kid, was impressed.

'After that it's the bulldogging event, and last of all comes the bronc riding,' Sandy told him. 'Then back home to Half-Moon Ranch for a cook-out by Five Mile Creek.'

Brett Lavin nodded and switched his gum from cheek to cheek. His father, Dale, told him to stay put while he went to place a bet on his favoured team for the wild horse race.

Amidst the excited chatter and the people milling about, Kirstie kept her eyes on the empty corral beyond the arena. 'What happens to the mustangs after the race?' she asked Hadley in a quiet voice. It was a question she'd never considered in the four years she'd been living at the ranch.

'They end up down at the sale barn,' the wrangler explained, as he nodded to a couple of old friends, tall, skinny men in checked shirts and stetsons like Hadley himself. 'If they're lucky, a rancher like Jim Mullins at Lazy B, or Wes Logan up at Ponderosa Pines will pay good money for them, break them in and use them as working horses on the cattle round-ups in spring and fall.'

'And if they're not lucky?' Lisa cut in.

Hadley shrugged. 'Some of these ex-rodeo horses are real mean. There's not a lot you can do with 'em.'

As Kirstie weighed up his answer and the uncomfortable silence that followed, she frowned. 'They wouldn't be mean if they were allowed to stay out in Wyoming where they belong. No horse is *born* mean!'

Brett Lavin had latched on to what he sensed might be an argument between the old ranch hand and the boss's daughter. He clicked his gum between his teeth and stared intently.

Sandy caught Kirstie's eye and gave a small shake of her head. 'Not now!' she whispered.

'Hey, why don't we go over to the corral to watch them unload the horses from the truck?' Lisa suggested brightly, linking arms with Kirstie and dragging her away.

'Am I right?' Kirstie insisted as the two girls threaded their way through the crowd. 'Do you know any horse that's born mean?'

'OK, OK, don't yell at me!' Lisa cut through a group of cowboys who stood waiting for the result of the team-roping event. When the scoreboard flashed up the winners to another loud cheer, the men turned to shake hands. 'I'm on your side, remember.'

Though she had lived all her life in the small town, and her mother, Bonnie Goodman, ran the End of Trail Diner on San Luis's main street, Lisa spent a lot of her time at her grandfather's place in the mountains.

It was there, at Lone Elm Trailer Park, that Kirstie had first met and made friends with the red-haired girl during the Scotts' first summer at Half-Moon Ranch. They'd been nine years old and had swapped friendship bracelets at the end of the school vacation, before Kirstie had started her first term at San Luis Middle School.

Since then, at exactly the same point in the year, when the aspen trees were silver-green in the mountain valleys and the clear lakes sparkled under deep blue skies, the girls had ridden out to Hummingbird Rock and exchanged new bracelets. Four bracelets for four years of friendship.

'Sorry,' Kirstie told Lisa now, as they arrived at the corral where a large truck was backing in. Two men ran to the rear of the truck to lower a ramp, and before the girls had time to take in what was happening, a bunch of horses clattered down the metal slope.

Noise, sudden light, strange smells. The mustangs emerged from the trucks with nostrils flared and ears set back. They wore rough rope headcollars and trailed lead-ropes after them. There were greys and blacks, tan horses and sorrels, Appaloosas and paints, all with long, flowing manes and frightened eyes. They kicked and bucked as they came out of the truck, rearing up in the bright sunlight, their hooves flailing and thudding into the dust.

Holding her breath, half in horror at the conditions in which the horses had been kept, half fascinated by their wild strength and beauty, Kirstie stared.

Soon a second truck backed into the corral to deliver more horses for the race. The ramp went down with a clatter and the mustangs fled from their dark prison. They squealed and whinnied, heads thrown back, eyes rolling in fear. And this time, Kirstie fixed her gaze on one particular horse.

He was a beautiful bay stallion with a jet-black mane and tail; bigger than the rest and first out of the silver truck. And he was crazy. He bucked and kicked, twisted, spun round on the spot, head down, thumping the ground. The sun shone on his rich brown coat; his strong shoulders and rump rippled with muscle as he screamed out his protest at being torn away from his endless plains, his sea of grass, his wilderness, to be dumped here, inside this circle of wooden barriers and curious, staring faces.

'Say!' A spectator whistled and sighed at the sight of the magnificent horse. 'That's where I'd put my money if I was a betting man!'

'A real rodeo champion,' his neighbour agreed.

The horse reared and threw back his head just feet from where Kirstie and Lisa stood.

Kirstie couldn't take her eyes off the bay horse. She heard the men's amused talk, and wondered how they could treat it so lightly. She gasped as a wrangler darted towards the horse,

10

seized the fifteen foot lead-rope and began to drag him across the corral. The horse fought back, pulling his head away and almost wrenching the rope out of the man's hands. But he was hemmed in by other mustangs, all led by wranglers who crowded them towards the wooden chutes that led into the main arena. He was forced to go with the flow.

Then he was in a chute, a barrier came down behind him, and he was trapped once more.

'Look at him kick!' The man next to Kirstie had followed the progress of the big bay horse.

'Rodeo Rocky!' his friend added, chuckling at the wild horse's antics inside the squeeze. He gave him a name that seemed to suit his bucking, kicking tricks. 'Yeah, I'll put five dollars on that horse. Five on Rodeo Rocky; make no mistake!'

The starting-pistol had fired and the wild horse race had begun.

Kirstie's attention was glued on Rodeo Rocky as he bucked and kicked his way into the arena. She ignored the teams of men standing with saddles inside the ring, the fresh cheers, the announcements over the loudspeaker. She had eyes only for the bay.

Between her and Rocky was a fence. Men with numbers on their backs were running to catch hold of trailing lead-ropes as other horses charged and twisted, skidded and spun. Dust was rising, there was a terrible heat and a feeling of fear.

'Rocky was a lead-horse,' she whispered to Lisa through gritted teeth. 'You can tell he was in charge of the herd by the way he handles himself.'

The stallion stood his ground amidst the chaos. His ears were flat, his eyes were hard. Kirstie saw him curl back his lip and snake his neck to bite the cowboy who approached him. The man leaped back just in time.

'Grab the rope, Jake!' he yelled to one of his partners.

A thickset wrangler in black T-shirt and jeans managed to take hold of the end of Rocky's lead-rope and twist it around his waist. He dug in his heels and leaned back with all his weight as the horse reared and pulled.

'Jake Mooney's the anchor man in black,' Sandy Scott told the girls. 'He's the best there is.'

Kirstie hadn't heard her mother approach as the race began, but she didn't turn round. Instead, she

12

nodded and kept her gaze fixed on Rodeo Rocky.

'He's got Gary Robbins on his team as mugger.' Kirstie's mom put one foot up on the bottom rail of the fence and leaned forward.

The mugger was the man whose job was to take hold of the taut rope and ease his way along towards the struggling horse. Kirstie knew what would happen next; Robbins would soon grasp the horse around the neck in a head-lock then reach out and pinch the top lip hard. The horse would squeal with pain and, while the hurt was bad, the third team member would dart in with the saddle. Before the horse knew it, the cinch would be buckled under his belly, and the rider would be on his back.

'Gee, d'you see that?' a spectator cried.

Kirstie gasped and gripped hold of the fence.

Rocky had twisted his head free of the mugger's lock and strained against the anchor man. By now, other teams had saddled and mounted their horses. Robbins swore and moved in to try again.

This time he grappled and succeeded in squeezing the bay horse's lip. Almost buckling at the knees from the pain, the stallion didn't resist as the saddle was slapped over his back. Kirstie closed her eyes for a second, then forced them open. Now

13

the rider, Fenney Brooks, was up in the saddle, the mugger had released his grip and the anchor man flung the lead-rope into Fenney's outstretched hands.

'He's off!' the bystander yelled. 'Man, see that bay horse go!'

Man and rider were almost last out of the arena on to the track, but they were catching up fast. Fenney was digging in his spurs, the horse's stride was long. They ate up the ground between them and the leading horses.

'This is awful!' Kirstie groaned at the sight of the rider's spurs. She left her spot by the fence and ran along the front of the crowded stand to the spot where the horses would thunder across the finish line. She heard Lisa coming after her. 'Did you see that?' she cried.

Hundreds of yards away, across the far side of the dirt track, the wild horses bunched together round the bend. The riders steered with the lead-rope, wrenching their horses' heads to left and right, spurring them on. One rider on the outside of the bunch lost his balance and crashed to the ground, curling up to protect his head from the thudding hooves. The crowd oohed and aahed.

Then a brown horse went down, kicking up dirt as he went, falling on to his knees and rolling sideways.

'I know; I can't look either!' Lisa hissed. Like Kirstie, she'd hidden her face behind her hands. 'Was it Rocky?'

Kirstie shook her head and squeezed forward for a view of the finish. She jumped up and down, dodged heads, slipped to the front of the crowd. 'Here they come!' she breathed, almost choking at the sight of the horses thundering towards them. 'Rocky's leading . . . He's gonna win . . . Yes, yes, he is!'

Horses and riders flashed by in a blur of faded colour behind a cloud of thick dust. Kirstie glimpsed bay and black, silver spurs cutting into the flanks, the creak of saddle-leather, the raised arm, the whip . . .

There was a deafening cheer, more shouting and spurring as the slower horses finished the race. Riders slid from the saddle, muggers and anchormen ran to join them. Mooney and Robbins slapped Fenney Brooks on the back as he stood by his sweating, bleeding horse.

Slowly Kirstie released her pent-up breath. She

fought back the sob that rose high in her throat as she stared at the trickle of blood from the cuts in Rodeo Rocky's heaving flanks. Then she glanced up at the fluttering banner above his head as Brooks took the lead-rope and dragged him back into the arena to receive first prize.

The bay stallion pulled away. His head was high, his jaw rigid, his back arched. He stood below the white banner that flapped in the cold wind blowing off the Meltwater mountains.

'Keeping the Dream Alive!' Kirstie re-read the bold red letters.

She gazed again at the wild horse that had been torn from his world, trapped, tied and ridden to exhaustion. And, as she glimpsed the nightmare in his eyes, she swore to him that she would help.

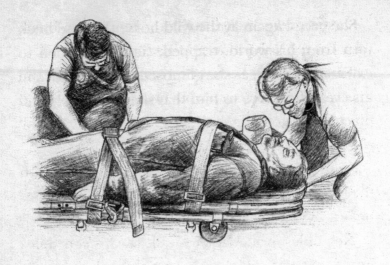

2

'One rider broke his jaw.' Hadley's report on the wild horse race was in full swing when Kirstie, her mom and Lisa rejoined the group from Half-Moon Ranch. Dale Lavin was smiling broadly and showing the other guests his winnings, while his son crowed in a loud voice over the way the cowboys had used their spurs to urge the mustangs on.

'You see that Fenney Brooks?' he cried, running to meet Kirstie and Lisa. 'I wanna ride like him, without a bridle. You see him? You see how he beat those other guys?'

Kirstie frowned and nodded. 'You wanna break your jaw too?' she muttered under her breath.

'Kirstie!' Sandy Scott stood between her and the guests. 'Why don't you and Lisa just find a good place to watch the bulldogging and the bronc riding? Meet us back here at half after four.'

Kirstie hung her head and scuffed the dirt with the toe of her boot. 'Do we have to? Can't we leave before the end of the show?'

'Not unless you want to walk the fifteen miles home,' Sandy said firmly, grabbing her by the shoulders and turning her away.

'I don't like to see it,' Kirstie complained. 'I can't stomach much more, Mom.'

Seeing she was serious, her mother kept one arm around her shoulder and walked her a little way off from the group. 'What's got under your skin, honey?'

The poor bay stallion, she wanted to say. *The cuts from the spurs; the look in his eyes.* But she was too choked to speak.

'Rodeo Rocky,' Lisa said quietly, coming up alongside Sandy and Kirstie and sticking out her chin in a determined fashion. 'We say that's no way to treat a beautiful horse!'

19

'I might agree,' Sandy replied. 'But what can we do? You saw how the crowd loved it. And the rodeos have been treating horses pretty rough for years and years. Are we gonna be the only ones to speak out?'

Kirstie took a deep breath and looked her mom in the eye. 'Yeah. Someone has to.'

'Then we'd be *real* popular with the ranchers and the rodeo organisers!' Sandy shook her head.

'So?' In Kirstie's mind, unpopularity was a price worth paying.

'So, we'd lose business,' her mother pointed out. 'Which we can't afford to do. We rely on people hearing good things about Half-Moon Ranch, to make them want to come and stay.'

'Your mom's right,' Lisa said after a pause.

Kirstie glared at her, as if to say, whose side are you on?

'Sorry.' Lisa shrugged helplessly and wandered off to watch the bulldogging event just getting under way in the main arena. There was a buzz in the crowd again, as the first riders galloped into the ring to either side of an angry steer.

Kirstie was left face to face with Sandy. 'Don't spoil the day,' her mother warned. 'I know it's hard, honey, but try and put a good face on . . . for my sake, OK?'

Out of the corner of her eye, Kirstie saw the bulldogger leap from his horse and wrap his arms around the thick neck of the bucking steer. Within seconds, the man had grabbed the bull's horns, twisted his head and flipped him sideways into the dust. 'OK,' she agreed. 'But I don't have to watch this. I'll be over by the corral if you want me.'

'Fine.' Her mom watched her go with a sigh, then went back to her guests.

At least if I wait by the corral I can watch the horses being saddled for the bronc event, Kirstie thought. Being with horses, anywhere, any time, was her main thing.

But today, even the pleasure of watching her favourite animal was spoiled by knowing that the wranglers were forcing saddles on their backs and dragging them into chutes. She felt a dull anger come over her as she made her way towards the corral and the scores for the bulldogging event went up on the board. Ignoring the cheers and the yells, she found a quiet corner where she could sit on the fence and wait out the rest of the afternoon.

Half an hour passed in a haze of dusty heat. The

21

cheers of the crowd sounded distant to Kirstie, whose gaze was fixed on the broncs in the corral. The unbroken horses milled restlessly in the confined space. One would break from the group and make a quick, nervy run towards the fence, spin and lope back. Another would raise his head and rear as a wrangler approached to cut him out of the herd. The cowboy would swing his lasso, the horse would feel the rope snake around his neck and burn into his skin as the man dug his heels in the dirt and pulled.

One horse, a fleabitten grey, gave her wrangler a hard time before she was finally forced into the squeeze. Too strong for one man, she jerked the cowboy off his feet and dragged him through the dust. Kirstie heard the man yell, saw two others race to help. They lassoed the grey mare's hind leg, then hobbled her by winding the rope around her neck, pulling the back leg forward off the ground. Then they dragged her, limping off-balance, into a chute.

'Gary, that fleabitten's your bronc!' a nasal voice yelled across the corral. The middle-aged speaker was a man Kirstie recognised with a shiver of dislike. It was Wade Williams, the owner and organiser of the San Luis Rodeo. He was tall and broad, with a sallow face and a heavy, dark moustache. 'You got that?' he shouted at Gary Robbins, one of the riders in the bronc event.

The cowboy strode around the outside of the corral, hat in hand, leather chaps flapping against his legs.

'You're first into the arena!' Williams instructed. 'Then Fenney on horse number 9!'

Kirstie sighed as the cowboys prepared for action. She saw Jake Mooney, the anchor man from the team-roping contest, speak with the organiser, who jerked his thumb towards the horse Mooney would be riding. She glanced in the direction of Williams' pointing finger, then stood up and clung on to the fence in dismay.

This couldn't be right. The stallion earmarked for the heavyweight cowboy was Rodeo Rocky!

Kirstie looked again to make sure. The bay horse trotted defiantly around the edge of the corral, his black tail swinging, the blood on his flanks now dry and congealed in long, dirty streaks. He wove in and out of the other horses, twisting and turning whenever a wrangler drew near.

'He's a tough one,' Wade Williams warned Jake Mooney.

'Yup.' Jake remembered the lead stallion all too well from the wild horse race.

'Think you can ride the buck out of him?'

'Sure,' came the careless reply.

As the men discussed Mooney's chances, Kirstie stepped down from the fence and drew nearer to the chutes. How could they think of putting Rocky through even more than he'd already undergone? Wasn't one cruel race enough?

It was because Rocky had shown such spirit in the first event, she decided. Williams must see him as a big crowd-puller, a real challenge even for the likes of Jake Mooney. With her heart sinking, her mouth feeling dry and her palms beginning to sweat, she watched the wranglers set to work on getting the bay horse into a squeeze.

And now events really did begin to blur and slide. As the lasso snaked around Rocky's neck and he reared up with an angry cry, the bulldogging contest came to an end and the first bronc rider was released into the arena. There was a wild cry from the crowd, a few seconds of tension as Gary Robbins kept astride the bucking, kicking grey.

'No!' Kirstie whispered, staring at the badly-cut bay stallion. A second wrangler moved in on Rocky to hobble him. The horse fought the lassos for all he was worth.

'Come away, honey,' a quiet voice at her shoulder said. 'If you can't stomach it, come and sit in the car.'

She turned to her mother. 'Mom, look what they're doing to Rocky. Make them stop!'

'I can't, Kirstie.' Sandy Scott took hold of her daughter's hand.

Over her shoulder, Kirstie saw Gary Robbins hanging on to the reins of his grey mare for dear life. One arm flung wide, head down, leaning back in the saddle, he rode the bucking bronc around the arena.

She turned back from the competition to the corral. 'Look! Now they're using an electric prod to force Rocky into the chute!'

Sandy grimaced. The metal prods were used on the ranches to manoeuvre cattle into the branding pens. As the electrified rod touched the bay's sore flanks, he whinnied and leaped sideways, into the path of a second wrangler, ready to pull the hobble rope tight.

At that second, a gasp and groan from the crowd told Kirstie and Sandy that Gary Robbins' bronc had finally succeeded in unseating her rider. There was a lull while the cowboy's time was recorded and he picked himself up from the dust. Now it was Fenney Brooks' turn on Number 9, a black and white paint.

Meanwhile, Rocky was prodded and forced into the chute closest to where the Scotts stood. The wranglers slammed the gate shut behind him, and one ran for the heavy saddle to make him ready for his turn in the competition.

Next, Kirstie saw Fenney shoot out of squeeze number 2 on the frightened paint. The slim, supple rider rode the horse's frantic bucks with ease at first, dipping and swaying, maintaining a perfect balance. Soon it would be Rocky and Mooney's turn, She groaned and half-closed her eyes as the wranglers slammed the saddle across his back and leaned through the gaps in the chute fence to fasten the cinch strap across the gashes in the horse's sides. How long now before Mooney jumped into the saddle and the chute opened?

But there was a delay. The crowd had stopped cheering. There were gasps and cries. A cloud of dust rose from the arena, and when it cleared, Kirstie could see Fenney Brooks down on the ground. He lay flat on his back without moving. The black and white horse, suddenly free of his rider, reared up over the lifeless body and thudded his hooves down within inches of the man's head.

Kirstie too gasped and ran towards the arena. In the eerie silence following the fall, she saw the wind catch Brooks' hat and roll it towards the fence. Then men were climbing the fence and running. One caught hold of the horse's reins to drag him clear. Another knelt over the rider, called for a stretcher and brought more helpers scrambling into the ring.

'It's crazy!' Kirstie whispered to Sandy, who hovered behind her. 'Mom, can't you see, this is all completely crazy?'

Without waiting for an answer, Kirstie ducked between the bars of the fence and ran into the arena. She saw Fenney Brooks stir and try to lift his head as a stretcher arrived. In the confusion, she was able to make it to the far side and grab hold of Wade Williams by the arm. 'You gotta stop them!' she yelled above the anxious swell of noise amongst the spectators.

Busy directing the rescue operation, the rodeo organiser tried to pull his arm free. When Kirstie hung on, he glanced round at her, his face red and angry, the corners of his mouth turned down beneath the heavy black moustache.

'They've used an electric prod on the bay stallion!' she cried. 'He's already cut from the earlier race. No way is this fair!'

The tall man frowned and pushed her to one side. Kirstie lost her balance and had to put out a hand to stop herself from falling into the dirt. Then she was up and following him across the arena to the squeezes.

Williams stopped short of Rocky's chute and turned on her. 'Quit it, will you?' With a quick look sideways, he gestured to Jake Mooney to get ready to mount his horse, which kicked and barged inside the trap. 'Soon as they've carried Fenney clear and got him into an ambulance, you're on!' he yelled.

The tough cowboy nodded and pulled on his black leather gloves. As he climbed the chute fence, poised ready to swing his leg across the protesting horse, his silver spurs clinked and glinted.

'Please!' Kirstie cried. She ran round to face the angry organiser. 'You have to stop this!'

'I said, quit it! Do you have any idea what you're asking?' His voice nasty and loaded with scorn,

Williams stood by Rocky's chute and stared down at her.

Kirstie held his gaze. She clenched her hands until her nails dug into the soft palms. 'Use another horse!' she pleaded. 'Rocky's hurt. Don't send him into the ring!'

The organiser sneered and shook his head. 'Come here, let me tell you something.' He leaned into the chute and roughly took hold of the bay stallion's reins.

Squinting into the sun, Kirstie saw Rocky pull away, eyes rolling, ears back. Above them, balanced on the top rung of the fence, Jake Mooney's black figure towered.

'What you gotta understand, little girl, is that this bronc is special,' Williams explained. 'He's strong, he's fast and he's mean. If we play our cards right, we'll make a champ of him!'

'What kind of champion?' Kirstie protested. She was stung by the organiser's insulting tone, but felt hot, dizzy and helpless before him.

Rocky strained away from the man's grasp, swinging his head, shaking his tangled mane.

'A prize bronc. We'll send him round the circuit; San Luis, Renegade, Marlowe County.'

Inside the narrow chute, Rocky reared and whinnied.

Williams held on to the reins, dragging the horse down. 'Then, in the fall, when he's got himself a big name as a bucking bronc, we'll truck him up to the Denver sale barn and sell him for thousands of dollars.'

Kirstie swallowed hard and bit her lip. She saw her mom quickly push her way to the front of the crowd, climb the fence and jump into the arena.

No way! she cried to herself, gazing up with tear-filled eyes at the struggling horse. *No way will we let that happen!*

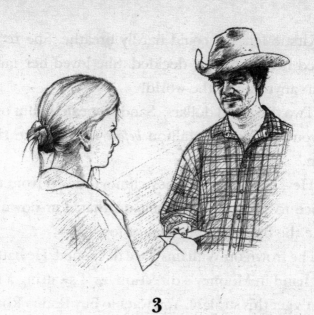

3

'I'll give you two thousand dollars for the horse.'
Sandy Scott's offer came across quiet and firm. Her
hand shaded her eyes from the sun's rays, which
caught her fair hair and made it shine the colour of
corn.

Taken aback, Wade Williams let go of Rocky's
rein. 'You can't be serious!'

'I've never been more serious in my life.' Kirstie's
mom didn't waver. She stood beside the chute, one
hand on the back pocket which held her cheque
book.

Kirstie felt she could hardly breathe. She really loved her mom, she decided. She loved her more than anything in the world!

'Two thousand dollars,' Sandy repeated. 'But only if you sell me the stallion *before* you let Jake ride him.'

'Hey, boss!' The cowboy climbed down from the fence to protest. 'You can't do that. I'm down to ride the bay. It's a big chance for me.'

The frown on Williams' face deepened. He batted his hand in Mooney's direction, as if swatting a fly. 'Let's get this straight. You want to buy Rodeo Rocky here and take him to work at Half-Moon Ranch?'

'You got it,' Sandy replied. She glanced sideways at Kirstie and gave a brief smile.

'Hm.' The rodeo organiser turned over the offer in his mind, while in the centre of the arena a team of paramedics worked smoothly to get the injured Fenney Brooks safely strapped on to the stretcher. The quiet crowd watched intently for signs that one of their favourite riders was going to make it through the accident.

'Well?' Kirstie's mother pushed for a reply.

'This is a great horse we're talking about.' Wade's tone had changed. The sneers had gone and he turned on the smooth talk. 'He has a good head and eye, and a mighty fine, deep chest.'

'Sure,' Sandy agreed. 'And two thousand is a good offer. You can take it or leave it.'

Kirstie squeezed her eyes shut. *Please, please, please say yes.*

'I reckon I could get two and a half thousand in the fall,' Williams said. A shrewd tone crept into his high, nasal voice and his eyes narrowed.

'Sure thing!' Jake Mooney encouraged.

'Maybe, maybe not.' Sandy Scott was on a level with Williams when it came to making a deal. 'Sure you could if the horse does well on the summer circuit. But if he doesn't, you won't get more than a thousand for him in Denver. Whereas, if you do business with me, you take the nice fat cheque home with you tonight.'

'Hm.' Wade grunted and pulled nervously at his moustache. He glanced quickly at the saddled bronc, then along the line at other horses trapped in chutes, awaiting their turn in the ring. 'Take horse number 12,' he snapped at Jake without looking at him, and reaching out a hand to shake with Sandy over the deal.

Yes! Kirstie raised her clenched fists in front of

her. Then she ran to the bay stallion and leaped on to the fence. 'We bought you!' she cried. 'Mom paid a fortune. You belong to us!'

The cheque written, the show went on without Rodeo Rocky.

'I sure as hell hope this cheque don't bounce!' Wade Williams sneered at Sandy as he pocketed the cheque.

'It won't.' Kirstie's mother was already looking round for help to take the stallion out of the cruel chute and get him fixed up for transport back to the ranch. Lisa had watched the sale of the horse from the edge of the arena and had volunteered to run and find her grandpa to see if he could oblige.

'D'you know what you've taken on here?' Williams couldn't resist talking down to Sandy. 'It don't take a lot of savvy to figure out that you've just bought yourself a whole bunch of trouble.'

'But you just said yourself that Rocky was a great horse!' Kirstie protested. In the background, she could hear the yells start up as, in place of Rocky, Jake rode a pure white horse into the arena.

'Sure: a great *rodeo* horse.' Williams stepped aside to let Kirstie and Sandy get a full view of their bargain. Inside the chute, Rocky still kicked and battered himself against the bars of his cage. 'Meaning wild and mean.'

'Only because he hated it in the truck!' Kirstie claimed. 'And because he's been tied up and prodded and forced to do what he doesn't want to do!'

'Yeah, sure.' Satisfied with the deal, the organiser shrugged. 'Come back and tell me that in a couple of weeks, after you've tried to break him in.' He turned his back and strolled off, leaving them to back their horse out of the squeeze and deal with him as best they could.

'Don't listen to him!' Kirstie told Sandy.

Hadley was nowhere to be seen, and they were still waiting for Lisa to show up with Lennie Goodman and a solution to the ride home with Rodeo Rocky. Meanwhile, two of the wranglers had stepped in to help them back the wild horse into the empty corral. After a few difficult minutes, they'd succeeded in getting close enough to open the back gate of the chute and let him find his own way out. Rocky had backed up, kicking and writhing, then lashed out with his heels when he found himself free of the trap. He'd run himself to a standstill round the corral and stood now, breathing heavily, covered in flecks of sweat, at the other side of the corral.

'We've got our work cut out,' Sandy murmured, looking him over with a practised eye.

'But we'll do it!' Still brimming over with joy that they'd saved the stallion from the rodeo, Kirstie wouldn't let doubts cloud her day. She looked round eagerly for Lisa's return.

'It'll mean tightening our belts for the rest of the summer,' her mother warned. 'We paid more than we could afford. Maybe we'll even have to sell one or two horses in the Half-Moon ramuda to make up some of the money.'

Kirstie only half-heard. She'd spotted Lisa and her grandpa pushing through the crowd to join them.

'Still, we made the decision,' Sandy said more firmly. 'And I'm glad. Rocky's a fine horse!'

'A *great* horse!' A smile spread across Kirstie's face as she spoke the words. A beautiful, free-spirited wild stallion with the wide open plains of Wyoming in his blood and a dream of liberty in his head.

* * *

'That's sure good of you, Lennie.' Sandy Scott gladly accepted the trailer-park owner's offer of a lift home for Half-Moon Ranch's new horse.

'Lucky I drove down with the horse-trailer,' the old man told her, keeping a wary eye on Rocky as he backed the pick-up truck through the gate of the corral. 'I brought it for a friend to do some business at the sale barn tomorrow, but I sure don't mind helping you folks out.' He leaned out of the driver's window and jerked his grey head towards the mustang. 'I hear you paid out a lot of money for this guy?'

As Sandy, Lisa and Kirstie got to work unbolting the trailer ramp, Sandy explained how the surprise deal had come about. 'We plan to work with the horse for a few weeks, get him used to the others in the ramuda, put a saddle on his back and gradually train him to be part of the trail-riding team.'

'But first you got to get him home.' Lennie jumped from the cab and took a good look at Rocky, who had raised his head and tensed up at the sight and sound of the truck and trailer. Lisa's small, wiry grandfather kept his distance while he decided how they were going to persuade the horse into the box.

'Are you gonna leave that saddle on him?' he asked.

'We've no choice,' Kirstie told him. 'We can't get close enough to take it off.'

'No problem. Hadley or Charlie can bring it down to Wade tomorrow.' Sandy rolled back her sleeves and began to move quietly towards the horse. 'Easy, boy,' she murmured, stopping to wait a while as Rocky pawed the ground then reared up. His lead-rope swung loose, the end knocking against his legs as he landed.

As they waited for the horse to settle, Kirstie spotted Hadley standing quietly by the gate. He'd been showing the Half-Moon guests around the rodeo grounds, but now she stole over and drew him to one side to give him the good news. 'Look what we bought for the ranch!'

'Yeah, I heard.' The old ranch hand scarcely opened his mouth to reply. He studied the stallion with narrowed eyes. 'Reminds me of a saying my first ranch boss used to have way back,' he muttered. 'Old Wes Douglas. His number one rule was, "A horse is a dangerous machine. You hurt him first, or he'll hurt you." '

'Oh, no way!' Kirstie shot back. The idea of inflicting more pain on Rodeo Rocky went against everything she felt and believed.

'You got some other way of showing him who's boss?'

She flicked her hair back from her face. 'Maybe.'

Before the argument with the old wrangler could develop, Kirstie went to help her mother. Sandy had edged in towards the bay stallion and reached forward, slow and smooth, to grasp the end of the lead-rope which trailed along the ground. She stood up without tightening it. 'Good boy!' she breathed.

Rocky's eyes rolled as he breathed in Sandy's smell. He backed off into a corner, pulling the rope taut as he went. The second he realised she was holding it, he jerked his strong neck and whipped it from her hand.

'OK, I could do with some help,' Sandy called, giving up the patient approach. Soon the corral would be needed again, so they would have to work faster to get Rocky out.

Hadley and Lennie moved up alongside her and Kirstie, keeping the horse pinned against the fence. Though Kirstie didn't like it, she had to stand by as Hadley beckoned a couple of rodeo workers to join them with lassos at the ready. Almost before she knew it, the ropes were thrown around Rocky's head and the struggle began again.

The stallion kicked and strained. He skittered and twisted, reared up, then trampled the dusty ground.

'Bring the truck up close!' Hadley yelled at Lennie, who ran to reverse the trailer.

'Stand clear!' Sandy warned the girls.

The men took the strain on the ropes as Rocky bucked and reared, the low rumble of the truck's engine sending him into another frenzy of defiance.

'Move him forward!' Hadley grunted.

'Yes, sir!' One of the rodeo men whipped the end of a rope down hard on the horse's buttock. The sudden pain shot Rocky forwards towards the lowered ramp. His hooves clattered against it, as once more, the man whipped him on.

Kirstie swallowed hard, longing for the episode to be done with. Soon, soon they would be able to set Rocky loose in Red Fox Meadow, by the cool, clear water of Five Mile Creek.

But meanwhile, he would have to endure the dark, stuffy trailer, the slam of the door as the ramp went up, the rocking and swaying of the journey home. Inside the metal box, the horse stamped and screamed.

'OK, let's go!' Sandy said quickly. 'Kirstie and Lisa,

you ride with Lennie. Hadley and I will follow with the ranch guests.'

As they sprang into action and Lisa ran round the front of the trailer to jump in her grandfather's cab, Kirstie paused long enough to catch a look pass between her mom and Hadley. She overheard a snatch of quiet conversation, before Lisa yelled for her to join them in the cab.

'. . . Don't look at me like that!' Sandy protested. 'I know what I'm doing.'

'What did I say?' Hadley shrugged as he slotted the last bolts of the raised ramp into place.

'You don't have to say anything. It's the way you look.'

The sceptical old ranch hand shrugged again.

'So, go ahead, say it!' Sandy challenged. 'Say what's on your mind.'

Hadley stood up straight, listening to the horse throwing himself around inside the trailer. 'OK,' he nodded, with a glance at Kirstie as she climbed into the cab. He spoke under his breath, so that she had to strain to hear. 'You want to know something? I think you just made a big – I mean a BIG – mistake!'

* * *

41

The round pen by the barn was empty except for Jitterbug and Lucky when Lennie Goodman pulled in through the arched entrance of Half-Moon Ranch. The other horses were out in the meadow, enjoying a well-earned afternoon's rest.

Kirstie's older brother, Matt, looked up from the work he was doing with the palomino and the sorrel. He quickly unhitched the lunge-rein from Jitterbug's halter, looped it over the white fence and strode across the yard to greet the truck as it parked by the gate of the pen.

'What the . . .?' Hearing the disturbance from inside the trailer, Matt stopped short.

'We'll tell you later!' Kirstie thrust open the door and jumped down. It had been fifteen miles of hell for Rocky on the twisting, rough road out of town along Route 5, almost an hour of torment for Kirstie and Lisa as they tried to block their ears to the horse's frightened squeals. Now they must unload him from Lennie's trailer and get him into the safety of the fenced pen.

Too busy to answer Matt's puzzled questions, she left her brother to Lennie Goodman and urged Lisa to help her lower the ramp.

'No, wait!' Lisa looked round the empty yard and

42

across at the barn. She yelled at a figure standing in the wide doorway. 'Charlie! We could do with some help!'

The young, dark-haired ranch hand threw down a rake and came running. When he reached the trailer and peered inside, he gave a low whistle. 'Wow!'

'Let's get him out!' Kirstie pulled at the heavy bolts, anxious to free Rocky from his ordeal. 'Open the gate, Charlie.'

Charlie Miller swung into action without asking any questions. He set the open gate to form a barrier that would stop the stallion from running off across the yard, then he ran round to the far side of the trailer to join Lennie and Matt, who were by now ready for the horse to come out. Once they were in place, Kirstie slid the last bolt free and lowered the ramp.

Rocky reacted to the sudden light and rush of fresh air into the box by ducking his head and charging. Out he came, clattering over the metal on to firm ground, past the three men and two girls, who stepped back to avoid his flying hooves. He sensed the sky above, the snow-capped mountains in the distance, the river water running through the valley. Freedom.

He was out of the trailer into the round pen, going wild, his rodeo saddle wrenched to one side, stirrups swinging wide, dirt flying from under his feet.

'Wow!' Charlie breathed. 'Some horse!'

'Watch out!' Matt yelled at Kirstie and Lisa, as Rocky raced around the edge of the pen, too close for comfort.

Driven crazy by forty-eight nightmare hours, the wild stallion careered towards Kirstie's own horse, Lucky, and the skittish sorrel that Matt had been working with when they arrived.

Jitterbug saw Rocky charge at her. Head high, dancing nervously in his path, she seemed not to know which way to turn.

'Get out of the way!' Once more Matt yelled a warning and waved his arms above his head.

Lucky took heed and trotted quickly to the far side of the pen. But the dainty mare froze as Rocky charged. The stallion bared his teeth, snatched at her neck and missed. He wheeled round, kicking savagely, striking out at the horse that stood in his way. The kicks landed with a thud. Jitterbug squealed and sank to her knees.

Seconds later, when Rocky had charged on and the dust had cleared, Kirstie saw the mare splayed out. Blood trickled from her nose. A dark red stain seeped slowly into the pale yellow ground.

4

The sun was low and red-gold over Eagle's Peak when vet, Glen Woodford, arrived from San Luis. Aspens and oaks rustled in the breeze on the banks of the creek, where a dozen ranch guests enjoyed the usual Thursday evening cook-out of barbecued chicken.

The visitors had arrived back at Half-Moon with Hadley and Sandy only minutes after Rodeo Rocky had brought Jitterbug down with his savage kick. Shocked at first, they'd quickly got over the incident, and were now relaxing outdoors, listening to Dale

Lavin play guitar as the sun went down.

'It's a good thing you called me out,' Glen told Sandy Scott as he examined the sorrel mare's cut face.

Kirstie stood in the background, behind her mother and brother, beside a subdued Lisa.

'She bled real bad!' Lisa whispered with a small shudder.

'Sure.' The vet cleaned the gash on the horse's nose with a white gauze pad. 'There's an artery runs right down this side, see. There's always a lot of bleeding when a blood vessel is damaged.'

Kirstie recalled how Hadley and Charlie had held Rocky at bay while she and Lisa had helped Jitterbug to her feet and out of the round pen into the nearby barn. She glanced down at her hands to see that they were streaked with dried blood from the sorrel's injury.

By the time Matt had run to the ranch house to call the vet, Sandy had driven through the ranch gates to be greeted by the chaotic scene. Just thirty minutes later, her mom had settled the guests and Glen had arrived.

'Who put pressure on the wound to stop the bleeding?' the vet asked, taking suture equipment out of his bag and injecting a local anaesthetic before he stitched the gash.

'Kirstie did.' Lisa gave her friend a worried smile. 'She didn't freak out, she just went ahead and did first aid until her mom got here.'

'That's good.' Glen Woodford worked quickly and skilfully, kneeling in the straw beside the injured horse. His closely cropped, dark hair was flecked with grey, his tanned face marked with fine lines under the eyes. 'It means she stands a better chance of a quick recovery. We don't need to give her a transfusion; just a few sutures, a shot of antibiotics, a top-up of sedatives, and she'll be just fine.'

'Poor Jitterbug.' Sandy crouched down beside the vet. 'I bet you never knew what hit you.'

As Glen finished his work and clicked his bag shut, he looked round at the watching group. 'So where's the brute who did this?'

'Still in the round pen,' Matt reported, his face lined with a deep frown. 'I cleared Lucky out of there real quick, but the bay made it plain he wasn't going anywhere.'

'So let's take a look at him.' The vet led the way out of the barn and into the lengthening shadows of the corral. The round pen stood beyond the area where the horses were saddled and made ready for the daily trail rides, behind the long, low wooden tack-room.

'I don't reckon the bay was hurt,' Matt said in a cold, unsympathetic voice. 'Just too crazy to know what he was doing.'

Kirstie followed silently, unable to argue for Rocky. But she understood why he'd done it. 'I'd like to see how they'd all act if they'd been treated the way he was!' she muttered to Lisa.

'I guess.' The uneasy answer came as the two girls arrived at the pen.

The bay stallion stood in the deep shadow cast by the tack-room wall. His coat looked almost black, the whites of his eyes glinted eerily as he stamped his feet and tossed his head.

Glen Woodford leaned against the fence and took a long hard look. 'That's a fine, big horse,' was his first comment.

'But?' Matt prompted, guessing from the vet's tone that there was more to follow.

'But he's a horse with problems, that's for sure. See how he pushes his nose in the air, walks backwards, plays up every which way he can?'

They all observed Rocky's restless antics.

'What are you saying?' Matt's voice broke the silence.

'I'm saying, first you gotta keep this horse away from the others,' Glen told them firmly. 'The mean streak that made him kick out at Jitterbug could run deep. And second, you can try working with him the way you would with other mustangs; roping him and getting him used to bit and bridle. But don't go getting your hopes up too high.'

'Meaning?' Kirstie's brother gave her a meaning-ful look, making sure she got the message straight.

Glen Woodford sighed and took a long time to answer. He'd turned from the pen and begun to walk towards his Jeep, parked by the ranch house, before he delivered his final verdict on the stallion. 'You can try, like I said. You put in all the work; spend hours, days, weeks with the lunge-rein here in the round pen, but my guess is you still won't break this horse!'

'The point is, we don't want to *break* him!' Kirstie insisted. Deep down she felt that the vet had been wrong about Rodeo Rocky.

The Scott family sat around the kitchen table with Hadley and Charlie. Lennie and Lisa had left them arguing over the day's events and driven on to Lone Elm. Now the door on to the porch stood open to let in the cool evening air. Kirstie watched the tiny hummingbirds hover round the birdfeeder in the dim dusk light, seeing them dart their long beaks into the honeyed water in the dish.

'So tell me how you plan to work with the horse if you don't want to break him?' Matt pushed aside his empty plate and leaned his elbows on the table. 'No, don't tell me. I don't have six hours to listen right now.'

Kirstie screwed her face into a frown. There was no point arguing with her brother in this mood. She looked to her mother for support, but Sandy Scott sat silent and worried.

'You paid two thousand dollars for a horse no one can ride!' Matt repeated a sentence he'd muttered several times during supper.

Across the table, Hadley caught his eye and shrugged.

'Give him a couple of days,' Charlie Miller broke in quietly. They were the first words he'd spoken, either during or after the meal, and he came across shy and awkward as usual. Until January of that year, Charlie had been a college student with Matt in

Denver. But he'd grown sick of the city and the rat-race and decided to take time out by working as a wrangler on the Scotts' dude ranch. He'd learned the job quickly under Hadley's guidance, showing skill at handling the hard-working quarter horses and mustangs, and leading the trail-rides with quiet confidence.

'It'll take more than a couple of days,' Matt objected, reminding them of Glen Woodford's verdict on the problem horse.

Sandy sighed and scraped back her chair as she stood up. 'This isn't getting us anywhere. On the one hand, Glen knows what he's talking about better than most. And you too, Hadley. I respect your judgment.'

Kirstie's heart sank as she listened to her mom. If the experts were against Rocky, what future did he have here at Half-Moon Ranch?

'On the other hand, I did make a decision back there. OK, so it was a spur of the moment thing, but I reckon I know a good horse. And you have to agree, this is a great-looking animal!'

Kirstie sat up and nodded. She found she was holding her breath as the family conference moved on.

'Maybe we should give him a chance,' Sandy said slowly, gazing out at the hovering, darting birds.

'Or maybe we should cut our losses and send him to the sale barn right now.' Matt didn't mean to be harsh, but he made it clear that he and Hadley were the only ones talking sense. 'If not, we put the other horses at risk, just like Jitterbug today.'

'And the guests,' Hadley put in. 'You put a dude on that bay stallion, he bucks him off, the guy breaks a leg. Then you kiss goodbye to your good name.'

'Good point,' Matt agreed. 'Honest to God, Mom, it'd be crazy to even try!'

'Hmm.' Sandy went to lean against the doorpost and gaze out across the corral at Red Fox Meadow beyond.

Kirstie followed her. 'A couple of days for him to settle down, Mom,' she said quietly. 'Please.'

A new moon had appeared over Bear Hunt Overlook; a pale silver circle in a fading blue sky. Across the yard, in the round pen by the tack-room, the shadowy figure of Rodeo Rocky could be seen standing absolutely still, ears pricked, listening to the sounds of the mountains.

Sandy glanced down at Kirstie's earnest face. She

lifted a hand to smooth her windblown hair. 'OK,' she said softly. 'A couple of days. Let's see how we go.'

'I don't know a whole lot of technical stuff about horses,' Charlie admitted when he met up with Kirstie in the round pen early next morning. 'Compared with Hadley, I'm a rookie.'

'I don't care. I'm just glad you want to help.' Feeling sure that she and Charlie were on the same wavelength, Kirstie zipped her red fleece jacket up to the chin and tucked her hair inside the collar. At the far side of the pen, Rodeo Rocky kept his wary distance.

'I reckon you have to stay back and just watch a horse before you try to get to know him,' the young wrangler went on. 'Give him a chance to decide you're OK, and no way are you gonna hurt him.'

'Me too.' She grinned at Charlie. 'See Rocky watching us now. Most people would move right in before he's ready, and start putting a rope around his neck and lunging him. I don't like that. Not until he's happy about it.'

Charlie grunted and nodded in Rocky's direction.

'Look at him lift his tail and high step around the pen!'

The stallion had decided to take a look at his two visitors. Instead of keeping the furthest distance from them, he began to trot in a circle which went round behind their backs about five metres from where they stood. As he trotted, he kept one ear pointed forward, but his inside ear was flicked towards Kirstie and Charlie.

'At least he's OK about us being in the pen with him.' Kirstie let Rocky trot round and round, head up, ear constantly flicking in their direction. 'That's one step up on last night.' She recalled the screams of anger and fright as they'd unloaded Rocky from the trailer, the way he'd lashed out at poor, unsuspecting Jitterbug.

The first rays of the sun caught the horse's dark bay flanks, giving his coat a coppery sheen.

'What do you reckon, fifteen hands high?' Charlie asked quietly, happy for Rocky to tighten his circle and trot closer in to where they stood.

'Maybe more.' Kirstie didn't feel a grain of fear as the stallion moved in. She thought it was wonderful the way his coat shone with the metallic gleam. It made him special, let him stand out from other normal bays. And the black mane and tail gave a contrast. Once they were combed through and the coat was brushed and groomed, Rocky would be the finest looking horse in the ramuda. 'It's amazing!' she sighed. 'Twenty-four hours ago, this horse was going through the worst time of his life. Locked up, tied up, shoved and prodded. You'd think it'd make him hate the sight of us.'

But no. As they stood quiet in the long, cool dawn shadows, Rocky was dipping his head and tightening his circle. *What's this?* he was asking them. *What do you want?*

He came closer, slowing to a walk, still moving in a cautious circle but ready to talk.

Then, across the neighbouring corral, the tack-room door opened and Hadley stepped out with a heavy saddle. The door flapped and banged against the wall as the old wrangler called out to them. 'Charlie, time to fetch the horses in from the meadow!'

As if reacting to an electrical current, the sudden noise made Rocky veer away from his patient observers. He swung out to the edge of the pen, loping at high speed in wide, reckless circles.

Charlie sighed and shrugged. 'Sorry.'

'That's OK.' Kirstie knew he was paid to take orders from Hadley. At least they'd had a few quiet minutes of making friends with Rocky. She smiled at Charlie as he fixed his pale straw stetson firmly on to his forehead and went to do his first job of the day.

And things are better than yesterday, she decided. She left the round pen as smoothly and silently as she could. Meanwhile, Rocky loped on, pushed by his instinct to flee at the first sign of danger.

Once through the gate, Kirstie turned to watch him run. Yesterday, Rocky had fought anything that went near him. Today he'd let her and Charlie stand in the pen. Yesterday, he'd been full of hate. Today he was curious, questioning, thoughtful.

It was a small step forward. But it was a step all the same.

'How's it going?' Sandy asked as she crossed paths with Kirstie on her way out to the corral.

'Good!' Her head was up, shoulders back as she went into the ranch house for a quick breakfast of blueberry muffins and coffee.

5

'How's the rodeo horse?' Brett Lavin asked Kirstie over lunch, his mouth full of hamburger and fries.

'Good!'

'How's it going with the bucking bronc?'

'Has he kicked any more horses in the face yet?'

The questions had come thick and fast as ranch guests came out of their cabins, criss-crossed the yard and rode out on the trails.

Kirstie had spent the morning on the ranch instead of taking Lucky out with one of the trail groups. Her plan was to hang around in the yard and the corral, where Rocky would be able to see her come and go. He would learn to recognise her from a distance, watch her at work, see her riding quietly by on her palomino as she took him to drink at the creek. With the guests out trekking towards Miners' Ridge or Elk Rock, the place was peaceful, with nothing to disturb the lone stallion in his round pen.

'So how's it going?' Sandy Scott wanted to know after lunch. She'd just come out of the barn where she'd checked on Jitterbug's cut nose, and was rushing to head up the afternoon ride through Fat Man's Squeeze to Deer Lake. But she stopped for a moment outside the tack-room to get a real answer about the problem horse out of her non-committal daughter. 'Come on, Kirstie, give me the low-down!'

'Better than yesterday.' Out of the corner of her eye, she noticed Rocky standing by the fence, looking out at the bunch of horses saddled and waiting in the corral. The clink of bridles and squeak of leather as riders mounted had caught his attention, and he stood alert and puzzled.

'Have you tried him on a lunge rope?' Sandy asked.

'Not yet. He needs more time.'

Her mom mounted Johnny Mohawk, a pretty, high-spirited, half-Arabian horse whose black coat shone in the full force of the afternoon sun. She swung her leg easily over the saddle and sat looking down quizzically at Kirstie. 'How much time?'

'Couple of days.'

'Sunday? Then, no doubt a couple more days after that. And before you know it, the horse has been living in the pen a whole week. You realise we need the space for Yukon's foal as soon as she gives birth.' Sandy reminded her that their six-year-old brown and white mare was in the late stage of pregnancy, and that both mother and baby would take priority in the pen.

'That's OK. Rocky will be ready to move into Red Fox Meadow by then,' Kirstie assured her, not letting her mom see that this was a pressure she could do without. Behind her cheerful front, Kirstie couldn't yet see a realistic prospect of letting the wild mustang loose.

And as Sandy rode the guests off to the lake under the bluest of blue skies, Kirstie chose a firmer approach for the afternoon. She would go into the round pen, she decided, but not with a halter and a lunge rope. They would remind Rocky too much of yesterday's rodeo. There would just be herself and the horse.

'Good luck!' Charlie passed by on Moose, a big, grey quarter horse, as Kirstie swung open the gate into the round pen. He gave a long look over his shoulder, then loped on to catch up with Sandy's group.

The gate clicked behind her and she stood, relaxed as she could manage, waiting for Rocky to get used to her entrance into his private ring.

The horse gave her his full attention. His tail swished from side to side, he stamped the ground once.

Kirstie took a couple of steps towards him, then stopped. She looked up at Eagle's Peak, across at the ranch house; anywhere but in Rocky's direction. But she could judge where he was by sounds. He'd begun to trot. Round the rim of the pen he came, one ear straight ahead, one ear flicked towards her. He snorted and ducked his head, kept on trotting.

Still Kirstie pretended she wasn't paying attention. She wandered a few steps to her right, then to her left, turned around on the spot, waiting for the moment when curiosity would get the better of the horse.

And sure enough, his circle grew tighter, as it had before breakfast that morning. It was Rocky's way of asking a question; *What do you want?*

Nothing. She let him know her answer by turning her head away. *No pressure.*

So, come on, what do you want? He slowed down, came closer.

Kirstie could feel the heat from his body, his warm breath on her bare arms. He was reading her body language the way she wanted, sensing that, far from being a threat to him, she was here to make friends.

And now he stopped and lowered his head, poking his nose towards her as she stood in the centre of the pen. He nudged her arm. *Come on, you must have some reason for being here.*

Kirstie felt a thrill of excitement. Here was this crazy, untameable horse coming up to her and giving her a friendly shove; the savage horse that only yesterday had kicked and bucked and bitten. Keeping a wide smile on her face, murmuring soft words of encouragement, she reached out her hand to stroke him.

* * *

'Wow!' It was Saturday morning, and Lisa had dropped in at Half-Moon Ranch with her mother, Bonnie. She was leaning on the fence, watching Kirstie work with Rodeo Rocky.

Less than two days in, and Kirstie felt she was well on the way to winning the horse's trust. True, he would still sometimes shy away when she walked into the pen. His ears would flatten and he would quickly put the biggest possible distance between them. But mostly he would allow her into the pen, take his time, then wander towards her, head lowered, licking his lips in friendly greeting.

'How do you do that without a lead-rope?' Lisa wanted to know as she watched Kirstie rub Rocky's face and shoulders.

'I don't know. It kind of happens, I guess.' She'd followed her gut-feeling that the horse must not be forced. When he was good and ready, he would come up and talk.

She proved it now by running her fingers down his strong, supple neck and listening to him snort with pleasure. Still she took care not to stare directly at him, knowing that, like all horses, Rocky would take this as a threat. And she'd learned how to move when he was around; slow and smooth, sideways and in circles, never fast and direct.

'How long did it take?' Lisa was obviously impressed. She gestured for Matt to get up from the porch swing where he was reading a book and come and look.

'A lot of hours. And we're not completely there yet. He *thinks* he can trust me, but he still has to be sure!' Kirstie showed her friend how she could sometimes drop her hands to her side, walk a few steps away and have Rocky follow her of his own accord.

'What do you think?' Lisa turned excitedly to Kirstie's brother.

'So far, so good,' he conceded, ready to wander back to his book.

'Isn't Kirstie cool?' Grabbing his shirt sleeve, Lisa insisted that he stay to watch. She shone a bright smile at dark-haired, good-looking Matt. 'Would you believe she could do that so quick?'

Matt shrugged. 'Yeah, yeah. But you wait till she tries to put a bit in his mouth and a saddle on his back.'

'Party-pooper!' Lisa pulled a face and turned back to Kirstie, who was letting Rocky nuzzle softly at the palm of her hand. The horse was blowing and

nibbling, nipping at the hem of her T-shirt, following everywhere she went. 'Take no notice of Matt!'
Lisa called. 'It's a guy-thing!'

'What's a guy-thing?' Kirstie walked slowly
towards her friend with Rocky in tow.

Lisa grinned and leaned over the fence to say
hello to the stallion. 'Matt knows he was wrong
about this horse,' she explained. 'And guys don't
like that. They like to be right!'

Sunday afternoon. Sandy Scott had seen off the old
guests at Denver airport and was driving back to
Half-Moon Ranch with a bunch of new visitors for
the start of a fresh week of trail-rides, cook-outs,
singalongs and quiet evening walks by the side of
Five Mile Creek.

Kirstie had stayed behind to work with Rocky
because Yukon was expected to foal tonight and
that would mean taking the stallion out of the round
pen and letting the new mother look after her foal
in safety. Yet Kirstie mustn't let Rocky feel that they
were under pressure. The horse had to be willing
to leave the pen and join the others in the meadow.

'Get Hadley or Charlie if Yukon shows any signs
of going into labour,' Sandy had instructed before

she left for the airport, knowing that Kirstie would be the one closest to the barn where the pregnant mare was stabled.

But so far, all was quiet. Matt was in San Luis visiting his girlfriend, Lachelle Jordan. Hadley was holed up in his bunkhouse, enjoying the few slack moments that his job allowed, and Charlie was the only one around to watch Kirstie's afternoon session with the rodeo horse.

'I'm gonna try him with a halter and lead-rope,' she decided after half an hour of the friendly stuff that Rocky by now so obviously enjoyed. The horse was happy to let her stroke and pat him from head to toe and had no thought of fleeing or playing up in his handsome head. 'We have to get a rope on him to lead him out to the ramuda when he has to leave the pen.'

Charlie nodded and went into the tack-room. Moments later, he emerged with the rope and harness and quietly handed them over the fence to Kirstie.

'This is your first big test,' she told the horse softly, letting the rope and collar hang unnoticed, as she hoped, from her right hand.

But Rocky had spotted the equipment. He tensed

up and backed off, then craned his head to sniff at the rope.

'Trust me, it doesn't mean we're gonna tie you and beat you up like Wade Williams' men,' she promised, swinging the collar towards him to let him get a proper sight of it now. 'It's what we do round here to get a horse from A to B. No pain involved, no problem.'

Charlie grinned. 'I sure hope he can understand what you're saying!'

Kirstie smiled back. 'Every word! Can't you, Rocky?' She offered him the halter to smell and explore. Then after a while she made her move, doing her best to look more confident than she felt. 'Now this slips on over your nose, like so.'

The horse blinked as the harness slid over his face. *Easy, easy; please don't fight it*! And that was it. The buckle was fastened, nice and easy. For the first time since he arrived at the ranch, Rocky was wearing a headcollar.

That night, when the new moon was high, Sandy Scott called Kirstie from her bed to come and watch Yukon's foal being born.

'Any moment now,' she promised as they crossed

the yard and entered the barn. They passed by a row of empty stalls until they came to a well-lit, straw-lined one at the end. The stall was fourteen feet square, giving plenty of room for the brown and white broodmare, while her helpers, Charlie and Hadley, stood outside at the ready.

'How do we know it's about to happen?' Kirstie whispered from outside the stall. The birth of a foal was a rare event on the ranch, since Sandy usually bought three-year-olds from the sale barn, ready to be trained and ridden.

'Yukon's been restless all day,' her mom explained. 'She's been lying down, getting up, biting her flanks and so on. Then, about an hour ago, her contractions started.'

Rubbing her eyes which were still prickly from sleep, Kirstie stared.

'This is it,' Hadley murmured. His expert eye had caught sight of the foal presenting itself in the birth canal. He showed Kirstie a pair of small front feet, explained that the foal would be in a diving position. The feet should soon be followed by the nose, neck and shoulders.

'Don't we help or something?' she whispered.

'No, she's doing fine,' her mother told her. 'We

only step in if there's a problem.'

Already the foal was slithering on to the hay, safely delivered by the mare. Then it rolled and wriggled inside the birth sac, breaking through and beginning to breathe of its own accord. As it did this, Kirstie found that she let go of her own held breath. She gave a deep sigh of relief.

'Now, the foal will try to get to her feet.' Hadley described the next stage. 'The cord should break and we treat the end with iodine solution. See, she's having a shot at standing up right now!'

Kirstie nodded. The tiny, fragile creature with its enormous head was wobbling up on skinny legs. Kirstie gasped as the baby fell and lay still.

'Too soon,' Sandy reported. 'Give her a few minutes' rest and she'll try again.'

Fascinated, Kirstie watched every movement of the newborn creature; the alert flick of her ears, the struggle to rise. Meanwhile, Yukon accepted her foal by licking her clean and nudging her on to her feet.

'When will she start feeding?' Charlie's eager question broke the soft, warm silence of the barn. It made Kirstie realise that this birth was the first the young wrangler had seen.

'In a couple of hours.' Hadley's easy, calm reply showed that he'd witnessed it many times. 'And come the morning, both broodmare and foal should go out into the round pen for exercise.' He turned questioningly to Sandy Scott.

Sandy nodded. 'I know. I warned you all that we'd have to move Rocky.'

For the first time since she'd crept out of her warm bed to watch the birth, a feeling of unease came over Kirstie. Sure, she'd known about the deadline, but she'd been pushing it to the back of her mind. She turned away nervously and pictured Rocky out there in his safe pen under the silver moon.

'That's OK,' Charlie encouraged. 'You can move him into the meadow, no problem.'

'You think so?'

'Sure. He's wearing a headcollar. He'll let you fix the rope and lead him out.'

Taking a deep breath, she nodded.

'Let Hadley do it,' Sandy suggested, picking up Kirstie's nervousness.

'No, that's OK.' Bad idea! There was only one person that Rocky had learned to trust. Kirstie knew it had to be her and no one else.

'Before breakfast,' her mom insisted. Satisfied that all had gone well for Yukon and her foal, she led the way through the dark barn out into the yard. They walked in the moon and starlight, by the round pen.

For a moment, Kirstie paused to glance over the fence. There was Rocky, awake and alert to the sound of their footsteps, keeping his distance, listening, looking. The copper gleam of his coat under the moon was weird, the black of his mane like a moving shadow, and the glint of his eye wary as his gaze followed their journey from barn to house.

'Tomorrow I'll take you to Red Fox Meadow,' Kirstie murmured to him through the darkness. 'It'll be fine, you wait and see!'

6

Rocky had to want to do it. Kirstie recognised the first rule about working with horses. If he wasn't willing to go into the meadow, nothing short of the extreme violence used by the wranglers at San Luis rodeo could make him.

'This is going to be OK,' she told him gently, choosing the first light of Monday morning when the sun peeped over the hills behind the guest cabins to go out into the round pen. With everyone except Hadley and Charlie still fast asleep, she knew there would be no distractions.

But she still had to convince the horse that she herself was calm and easy about the move. She had to enter the pen with halter and lead-rope as if there was nothing unusual, nothing threatening about to happen. There must be a smile on her face, the same casual, indirect approach as ever. As she drew near and looked up at his intelligent, sensitive face, she stroked his neck and murmured encouraging words. 'OK, you're doing great. I'm gonna slip this headcollar on and we're gonna walk right out of here into Red Fox Meadow.'

Slowly, with the shadow of suspicion gradually melting from his eyes, Rocky let her ease the collar over his nose and strap it behind his ears. He dipped his head and nuzzled her arm.

'Let's walk.' Giving the gentlest of tugs on the lead-rope, she set off for the gate.

The big bay stallion followed quietly, his coat gleaming, his dark mane blowing in the breeze. He scarcely looked at the gate as they stepped outside the pen into the yard, his ears forward, then twitching this way and that.

'*Goo-ood* boy!' Kirstie headed for the wooden bridge across Five Mile Creek. Beyond that lay the meadow, where Hadley and Charlie were already cutting out from the herd the horses that would be needed for the day's rides. 'This is gonna feel kind of strange,' she told Rocky, as their footsteps echoed on the thick pine planks that formed the bridge. 'You're gonna meet Cadillac and Crazy Horse out here. Cadillac's the big, creamy-white mustang and he knows he's beautiful, but don't let that bother you. Then there's Crazy Horse. Crazy Horse has to be the ugliest horse around, but he thinks he's a good-looking guy, just like Cadillac. You can't come between those two; they go every place together . . .'

As she chatted on about other horses in the ramuda, Kirstie led Rodeo Rocky along the side of the creek towards the long stretch of high fence that formed one side of the field where they kept the Half-Moon horses at grass. The field began broad and flat, then sloped upwards, away from the creek, and narrowed so that the whole shape was a six-hundred foot long, sloping triangle laid out at the foot of Hummingbird Rock. At the far end, she spotted Charlie on Moose, working to cut Johnny Mohawk out of the herd and head him towards the ranch.

She paused with Rocky at the wide gate into the meadow, beside a big clump of tall blue irises. The mustang sniffed at the flowers, ignored them and craned his neck to reach golden marsh marigolds growing closer to the banks of the fast flowing creek. As he chomped on the juicy dark green leaves, Kirstie saw Lucky trot across the meadow to greet her. The palomino's pale mane and tail swung as he came, his head was up, the sun shone on his golden coat.

Rocky turned at the sound of approaching hooves. For a moment, as his lip curled back and he bared his teeth, Kirstie feared a problem. Up till now, since he'd been kept alone in the round pen, she'd given Rocky her undivided attention. But Lucky was her special horse and no way was she going to ignore him for Rocky's sake. She wondered if it was possible for a horse to be jealous; if her talking to the palomino and making a fuss of him would throw Rocky into a mean mood.

She decided to tether his lead-rope to the fence-post just in case. He watched her carefully as she tied the slip-knot, then he eyed the palomino.

'Hey.' Kirstie stood clear of the bay horse and leaned over to say hello to Lucky. She rubbed his neck, then laid her cheek against his cheek. Then she stroked his nose and stepped back.

How had Rocky taken it, she wondered?

The bay stallion had his head up, his eye fixed on Lucky. He tugged at the rope, found he had nowhere to go and stamped his feet. Kirstie went back to him more warily than before. 'This is Lucky,' she told him, as the palomino approached them calmly from the other side of the fence. He was as tall and strong as the wild horse; a match if the two decided to fight.

Rocky flared his nostrils and whinnied loudly. He turned his head quizzically to Kirstie.

This is like being a new kid in school, she thought suddenly. *New kid doesn't know anyone, feels awkward and left out. Teacher details a confident, friendly kid from the class to help the newcomer settle in.* The comparison made her smile and relax. She went back to Lucky. 'Rocky's new here,' she explained, half-laughing now. It was crazy to talk to a horse like this, and yet she knew somehow that both Lucky and Rocky were getting the picture. 'He needs some help. I'm gonna lead him into the field to join the ramuda. You have to show him how, OK?'

Lucky leaned over the fence and snorted.

Quickly Kirstie went to untie Rocky's lead-rope. 'And we know you're a big, tough guy,' she told him briskly. 'But we don't want you throwing your weight around just to prove it.' She led him firmly to the gate, opened it and took him into the field. The horse looked at the small herd of fifteen ranch horses in the distance, glanced sideways at Lucky and dipped his head.

It was the moment for Kirstie to unclip the lead-rope. One smooth movement and Rocky was loose. She held her breath, watching every sign: the head, the ears, the eyes.

It was Lucky who made the first move. He came right on up to the powerful newcomer, wiggling his ears and blinking. For a split second Rocky held back, switching his tail, staring, telling him 'Keep your distance'. But Lucky ignored the message. He thrust his nose towards the bay horse, his sensitive nostrils sniffing, then breathing out noisily. Then he walked right round the back of him, saying, 'You could kick me if you had a mind to, but I don't think you're gonna do that.'

Quietly Kirstie watched and smiled. Lucky came full circle, back to Rocky's face. He made a trot away, came back, danced a bit, trotted again.

'Go!' Kirstie urged the new horse.

He waited a few more seconds, trying to decide.

Should he stay? Should he go? At last, he crouched back on to his haunches and launched himself across the meadow after Lucky. His hooves sank into the soft turf, his tail streamed behind him. Soon the two horses were thundering the length of Red Fox Meadow, matching each other stride for stride, as the rest of the herd stood quietly by.

'Neat!' Charlie said as he rode by with Johnny Mohawk, heading for the ranch.

Kirstie nodded with a satisfied grin. She slung the rope over her shoulder, shut the gate after Charlie and went to tell her mom: No problem, Rodeo Rocky was doing fine.

'Here's how I see it.' Kirstie helped at the cook-out by serving barbecued chicken to the guests and explaining her theory about Rodeo Rocky to anyone who would listen.

It was one week after the ex-rodeo horse had joined the Half-Moon ramuda and as far as Kirstie was concerned he'd been behaving like an angel. Now Sandy Scott, Lennie Goodman, Lisa and Matt were considering the transformation that had come over the big bay horse.

Kirstie spooned barbecue sauce over the plates,

then waved the ladle around. 'No horse is born mean. He only gets mean if someone treats him rough. So, with Rocky, he had one bad experience and it scared him real bad. For two days he went crazy.'

'Hey!' Lisa protested, as a splatter of barbecue sauce narrowly missed her clean blue T-shirt.

Kirstie ignored her friend. '*You'd* be crazy if you'd been kidnapped and forced into some dark truck that roared you away from the beautiful place you'd lived in all your life!'

'Sshh, honey!' Sandy took the sauce ladle from her and made her serve salads instead, hoping she could do less harm.

'. . . So!' Kirstie didn't even notice that she'd changed jobs, she was so excited about Rocky's progress. 'With Rocky, it was like all men are the enemy!'

'Sure.' Matt conceded this much. 'But you're saying you've worked with him and got rid of this crazy streak?' All week he'd remained doubtful, and it seemed he wasn't about to change his mind.

Kirstie nodded. 'He's smart; real smart. It only takes him twenty-four hours in the round pen to know all men aren't the enemy after all. He checks me out and decides I'm OK, for a start. I'm talking to him, I'm feeding him, I'm taking him out to the meadow and showing him where to find the best grass.'

'He knows you're with him, not against him!' Out of range of Kirstie's waving arms, Lisa gave her friend some warm support. 'Have you been out to the meadow to see him with the other horses?' she asked Matt and Sandy. 'The herd gives him respect because he's big and strong . . .'

'. . . Except for Silver Flash,' Kirstie put in. The big sorrel with the white blaze down her nose hadn't exactly given Rocky a warm welcome.

'OK, and poor Jitterbug wasn't too happy either,' Lisa admitted. 'But there's been no real trouble. Lucky made sure of that. He took to Rocky, showed him round real good.'

'Lucky's been great,' Kirstie agreed, drowning Lennie Goodman's salad in dressing. 'He stuck with Rocky. Now it's Cadillac and Crazy Horse; Lucky and Rocky. No one can get between those two any more!'

'Well, that's great.' Kirstie's mom was genuinely pleased. 'I've been checking Rocky out all week, and I agree with you, you wouldn't know him as the same horse as the one we drove up from San Luis.'

'So when does he start earning back what we paid for him?' Matt stacked used plates on a nearby table. 'Meaning, when do we put someone on his back and let him ride out on the trails?'

There was a pause. Kirstie cocked her head to one side and looked at her mother.

'Hmm.' Sandy set off indoors with the heavy stack of plates. 'One step at a time,' she insisted. 'We haven't even got a saddle on him yet.'

Kirstie and Lisa glowered at Matt for spoiling the mood. Kirstie knew her mom was still worried about the two thousand dollars they'd paid for Rodeo Rocky, and was still having to consider the possibility of selling Yukon and her tiny foal to make up for the two thousand dollars she'd spent.

'So?' Matt widened his eyes and shrugged.

'Soon!' Kirstie answered back. She turned around and walked away, down the green bank to the edge of the creek, where she gazed across at the horses in the meadow. She could easily pick out Cadillac's white form from the rest in the twilight, and shadowing him was ugly-beautiful, faithful Crazy Horse. Then beyond them was pretty, dainty Johnny

Mohawk, and beyond him the golden coat and pale blond mane of her precious Lucky. Sure enough, at his side she made out Rocky. He was turned away from the herd, head up, staring at the wild slopes of Eagle's Peak, as if his mind was soaring up there, away from the ranch to the pine-tree wilderness in the quiet evening air.

Kirstie saw him and sighed.

'When?' Matt had followed her to the river's edge and spoke quietly from behind. 'It's time to saddle and ride him,' he told her. 'So when will it be?'

A saddle on the wild mustang's back. A metal bit in his mouth. Reins to hold him back. It was the big, big step.

'Tomorrow,' she whispered. 'I'll give it a try.'

Yukon looked over the fence of the round pen as Kirstie chose a saddle and carried it out of the tack-room. The mare's eight-day-old, black foal skipped and bucked across the sandy ground on her spindly legs. Her large head with its white star wobbled up and down as she scampered across. Each day she grew a little bigger, a little steadier on her feet. And Yukon was a good mother, protecting her from the too-curious gaze of some of the ranch guests, standing over her when, tired out by playing and feeding, she folded her legs and took a nap in the sun.

Kirstie smiled at the mother and foal, hooked the heavy saddle over the corral fence, then walked on to fetch Rocky.

'We have to sell something!' Matt had insisted over breakfast. He said he'd been working on some figures late the previous night, and he couldn't make them add up to show a profit unless they took the tough decision to sell at least one horse.

'I hear you,' Sandy had said with a worried frown. 'And I know it's not looking good right now. But maybe we'll hit lucky with a late booking. If we got in some extra guests, that would solve the cash-flow problem.'

'Yeah, and it would solve the problem if we sold the rodeo horse,' Matt had said, looking pointedly at Kirstie. 'We'd get our two thousand dollars back; end of story!'

Kirstie had deliberately turned her back on him, put on her fleece jacket to keep off the chill of the morning dew, and come out for Rocky's saddle.

Saddle equals rodeo. Rodeo equals ropes, loss of freedom, pain. She predicted the train of thought inside

84

Rocky's head as she approached Red Fox Meadow. He would hate the sight of the polished leather and metal stirrups the moment he saw it. It would take all of Kirstie's calmness and courage to help him through this.

'Excuse me, Ma'am, can I get your horse for you?' Charlie's joking voice broke into her thoughts with the phrase he and Hadley used for the lady ranch guests. He was riding across the meadow towards her with Cadillac and Crazy Horse in tow.

'Oh, hey Charlie!' She gave him a small grin. 'Do you have time to watch me tack Rocky up?'

'When?' From his saddle, the wrangler watched the ex-rodeo stallion trot willingly to greet her.

She slipped a headcollar on to the bay horse and led him towards the gate, squinting into the sun that sat on the rim of the hills behind the cabins. 'Right now?'

'Sure thing.' Charlie said he would ask Hadley for a ten minute break, then join her at the round pen.

So Kirstie had Rocky inside the ring and was lunging him on a fifteen foot rein when Charlie joined her. 'He noticed the saddle slung over the fence,' she told him quietly. 'I let him sniff at it for a while. He seemed OK about it, but I don't know how he'll be when I put it on his back.'

'He'll be great,' Charlie told her. 'I'll take the rein while you fix his saddle.'

She took a deep breath. It was now or never. As Charlie slowed the horse from a trot to a walk, then reined him to a standstill, she approached with the saddle.

'That's right, nice and easy,' Charlie said softly, as Rocky's ears flicked and he bowed his head.

Kirstie lifted the heavy weight level with Rocky's shoulders. Her arms ached with the effort, but she didn't let the saddle drop straight down on the horse's back. Instead, she let him turn his head to look, waited until he'd agreed that it was OK to go ahead, then eased it on to the curve of his back. Gently, gently she lowered it until it rested comfortably in position.

'Easy, boy!' Charlie whispered. The lunge rein stayed relaxed in his hands.

'You're doing great!' Kirstie soothed. She didn't let Rocky see how keyed up she was as she lowered the cinch, took the strap under his belly and brought it up the other side. Before the horse knew it, the buckles were fastened and stirrups lowered.

Rocky shifted under the new weight and the feel of the tight cinch. But he didn't seem to seriously object.

'Good boy!' Now she praised him and patted him, rubbed his neck and shoulders, made a great fuss. 'Trot him round the ring while I fetch the bridle,' she told Charlie, dashing to the tack-room once more. As she unhooked a bridle from its peg, she saw Hadley and said he should come and watch. Then they bumped into Matt and Sandy in the yard. 'Everyone come and see this!' Kirstie insisted, running back into the pen.

And now she was confident that Rocky would trust her with the rest of the tack. She might even be able to ride him. But she mustn't be too eager. Slow and easy, she told herself. Charlie grinned at her and she grinned back as she approached the horse.

'Now this bridle is just like a headcollar,' she explained. 'There's a metal bar that slides inside your mouth, and a few straps around your face. I fasten it real simple, and the reins go over your head, like so.' Kirstie talked as she worked, conscious of her small audience standing at the gate.

Rocky shook his head and snorted. He felt the cold metal in his mouth; a strange sensation for the horse from the flat Wyoming plains. He turned to look at Kirstie with a big question mark in his eyes.

'This is so I can get up on your back,' she told him, keeping her voice calm and cheerful. 'Sure, I know it's a whole lot of fancy stuff and you'd let me on without it, but it helps me stay up there, believe me!'

'Try riding him,' Charlie urged.

Kirstie glanced at her mom, who hesitated, then nodded.

So Kirstie slid her left hand down Rocky's neck and took hold of a bunch of coarse black mane along with the slim rein straps. She bent her left leg and hooked her foot into the stirrup, then, holding on to the curved back of the saddle with her right hand, she heaved herself off the ground and slung her free leg over.

'Yes!' Charlie breathed.

She was in the saddle, looking down at Rocky's broad shoulders and long, coppery brown neck. He was skittering sideways, dancing a little, but not seriously misbehaving.

'That's excellent, Kirstie!' Sandy called across the pen.

'Cool.' Matt nodded his approval.

Hadley said nothing, as usual.

But as the old wrangler called Charlie to help him saddle the other horses in the corral, Kirstie could tell that even Hadley was impressed by the progress she'd made with the wild horse.

Taking a deep breath of fresh mountain air, she tightened the reins and tilted her heels down in the broad stirrups. Settled and balanced, safely astride, now she felt ready for whatever Rodeo Rocky might throw at her.

7

'You make the right things easy for the horse and the wrong things hard,' Sandy Scott told Kirstie. They were working with Rodeo Rocky in the round pen five days after the stallion had been successfully saddled and ridden. It was late evening; a time when tiny bats flitted overhead and the mule deer wandered down from the high slopes, stalked by shadowy grey coyote with their telltale howling cry.

'Meaning?' Kirstie left off teaching Rocky to respond to the reins and walked him quietly over to where her mom stood.

Sandy tilted her hat back and began her explanation. 'Well, you make the right things easy by making them fun. When Rocky obeys the rein to the right, you rub his shoulder and scratch his neck, do all the things he likes.'

'And if he gets it wrong?' Kirstie couldn't imagine that her mother was telling her to hit or punish him in any way.

'You hold back the praise and the fun. A horse likes the games you play with him when he gets it right. He likes them so much, it feels bad for him when it doesn't happen. So next time, he'll try to understand what you're asking him and do his best to get it right.'

'But I don't have fun with him until he does?' Kirstie set off with Rocky round the pen to try the reining technique once more. This time, the horse responded well, so she leaned forward to praise and pat him.

'That's real good.' Sandy too was pleased. She stood back and watched Kirstie work on until the light got too bad. Then together they unsaddled Rocky and led him out to the meadow, where Lucky stood at the gate waiting for him, his pale mane and tail picked out in the deepening dusk. Kirstie let Rocky loose and the two horses greeted each other then loped the length of the field.

'Happy?' Sandy asked Kirstie as they walked back to the ranch.

'Yep.' They crossed the bridge, noticing the lights go on in the cabins, hearing Hadley play his harmonica in the bunkhouse doorway. 'How about you?'

'Yep,' Sandy replied.

'So can I ride Rocky on the trail?' Kirstie waited for the reply for what seemed like an age. She felt he was about ready to try and begin work as a ranch horse, but would Sandy see it that way?

Her mom stepped on to the ranch house porch, took off her hat and shook her hair loose. 'Why not give Lisa a call?'

Kirstie ran ahead of her. 'Mom, what kind of answer is that? I was asking about trail-riding Rocky!'

'Sure.' A smile played about Sandy's lips. 'That's why I said you should give Lisa a call.'

'Huh? What's the connection?'

The smile broadened. 'I'm thinking Lucky and Rocky. They like to be together. And that makes me think you and Lisa. You get on pretty well too.

So if Lisa can make it tomorrow, and she wants to ride Lucky . . .'

'. . . That means I could ride Rocky and we could all go out on the trail!' Kirstie jumped in. 'Great idea, Mom!'

Flinging her baseball cap down on the porch-swing and dashing into the house to grab the phone before Sandy could have second thoughts, she went ahead with the arrangements for Rocky's biggest test of all.

'Excuse me, Ma'am, can I get your horse for you?' Charlie came up behind Lisa as she stood in line in the corral next day. He grinned sideways at Kirstie.

Lisa turned round. 'Hey, Charlie, it's me!'

'Wow!' The wrangler stepped back in mock-surprise.

Kirstie jerked Lisa's arm to pull her out of line. 'He's fooling. Come on, we're going with Hadley on the advanced ride.'

It was all arranged. Lisa's mom had driven her daughter up before opening-time at the diner. Lisa had arrived in new jeans and boots, wearing a native American necklace made from leather and tiny turquoise, white and black beads. 'We're not going on a fashion-shoot!' Kirstie had cried. 'We're trail riding up to Bear Hunt Overlook, remember!'

That morning she'd pulled on an old check shirt belonging to Matt. It was faded and torn. Her jeans were worn at the knees and rolled up at the bottom. 'It looks like those are mine too,' her brother had grumbled as she'd scrambled a breakfast of waffles and chocolate sauce.

'Don't mess up your new jeans!' Bonnie had called to Lisa from the old Ford pick-up truck she drove. The warning had drifted off on the breeze.

And now Kirstie was hurrying her friend over to the post where Lucky and Rocky were tethered because Hadley was ready to head his group of experienced riders out on the trail. There was no time to talk or worry about the ride ahead as they quickly mounted and followed the line of guests out of the corral and over the wooden bridge.

As the horses' hooves clattered, then came back on to solid ground, Lisa saw that Rocky was edgy and urged Lucky ahead. 'He'll follow if Lucky leads,' she called over her shoulder, urging the palomino into a trot and rising neatly in the saddle.

Sure enough, Rocky picked up his pace, ears forward, concentrating on Lucky, as Hadley took a trail that led to one side of Hummingbird Rock, and on through Fat Man's Squeeze to the giant overlook beyond.

Kirstie took care to praise him for settling down. Instead of pulling at the reins and dancing sideways, he went willingly, picking up his feet and choosing the surest, safest way through the bushes and between the rocks. Soon he was confident enough to put on speed and stride out alongside Lucky, catching up with the rest of the group just as the head wrangler was instructing them to split up and lope on past Hummingbird Rock.

'Meet up at the bunch of ponderosa pines,' he told the visitors. 'After that, there's a steep climb until we get to a narrow gulley. We do that part of the ride together, OK?'

The half-dozen riders nodded and went their separate ways, giving their horses their heads and loping across country. They ducked and dodged branches, jumped fallen logs, sometimes staying in the saddle by grasping the horn and clinging on as the horse charged ahead.

'You think you can do this?' Hadley stayed behind to ask Kirstie and Lisa.

They nodded and reined their horses round to

face the slope. Kirstie could feel Rocky's eagerness as he scented the keener air blowing from the mountain tops. When she squeezed his sides and let him go on, he surged away without even waiting for Lucky.

And they were off up the hill, thundering across the ground. Kirstie ducked to miss an overhanging branch, swept by the side of another, swayed in the saddle as Rocky swerved around a rock. Behind her, she could hear Lisa and Lucky close on their heels. Ahead, the dude riders had fanned out, each taking a different track to the finishing point by the pines. Like them, she arrived breathless and pleased.

'OK?' Lisa checked with Kirstie. The wind had blown her hair into unruly curls, the pretty necklace was crooked, but she had a huge grin on her face.

'Great. Rocky is fantastic!' She kept her voice low in case Lucky got upset and jealous. 'And so are you too!' she told him. The two horses jostled in the shadow of the pine trees, then got into line as Hadley checked that everyone was there.

'We're gonna go through the Squeeze,' he reminded them. 'It's a gulley between two cliffs. Some of the horses don't like it, but you let them know who's giving the orders and they'll do it, no problem.'

Kirstie knew the place. It was only wide enough for one horse at a time. To either side, the pinky-grey granite rocks rose sheer and bare. As she held back and set Rocky on the trail last in the line, she began to worry, and her edginess was picked up by the smart horse.

'OK?' Lisa turned to check again.

Rocky was falling behind, shaking his head and flattening his ears.

'He doesn't like the cliffs,' Kirstie answered. The shadows from the tall rocks had closed in, and by this time the first riders had entered the Squeeze. 'Tight spaces remind him of the rodeo chutes, I guess!'

'You want to turn back?'

'No. Let's try,' she decided. How would it look if she and Lisa rode back to the ranch early? They would have to give Sandy and Matt the reason, and admit that Rocky wasn't going to make the grade as a working horse after all. Not yet, at any rate, and time was short.

So they rode on into the gulley, Lucky stepping out first as if there was no problem, picking his way over the rocky ground, sure-footed and confident as ever.

Rocky watched him every inch of the way. Where Lucky went, he could go too. Though he was tense and tight, he battled with his fear and went on.

'Easy, boy!' Kirstie soothed him with her voice and helped him along. The track narrowed, the rocks rose high to either side. Inside the Squeeze the light was gloomy, the air damp, all sound deadened.

But Rocky made it through. Hating every second, flinching as he went, he came out the other side to join the group. Hadley gave Kirstie a keen, questioning look. She nodded, and without a word he carried on.

'Rocky's a grade A student!' Lisa sighed happily as the riders tethered their horses to tree branches on Bear Hunt Overlook. The others went ahead to sit at the edge of the rock and take in the spectacular view down the valley during their ten minute break. 'He just took his first exam and passed!'

Kirstie slid from the saddle and led Rocky to a vacant tree. The ride had taken more out of her than she was ready to admit. Her mind had been full of questions that she'd had to keep hidden, and the effort of telling Rocky not to worry, of keeping him on the trail with the other horses, had been hard on her. Now she felt pleased but tired, glad of the rest as she unhitched Rocky's tether rope and began to tie it to a low branch.

She was hurrying with the slip-knot in order to retrace her steps across the flat top of the overlook to rejoin Lisa and Lucky, when a sudden noise in a bush on a steep slope to the side of the tree stopped her. Rocky heard it too, froze and stared up at the rustling branches.

'Come on, Kirstie!' Lisa yelled, wanting to climb to the top of the overhang and join the rest of the group.

Her voice must have alarmed the creature crouched under the bush. The leaves shook, the branches parted, and out crawled a grey, silent shape.

'Coyote!' Kirstie cried. She recognised the wild dog in an instant, with its thick fur and long, bushy tail, its thin, pointed muzzle and slanting amber eyes that stared down at them from the rocky slope.

Before she knew it, the startled animal had crept free of the bush and started to advance. It was coming at her, lip curled back to show vicious canine teeth, a low growl deep in his throat.

'Get out of there!' Lisa yelled. Then she called for Hadley. 'Kirstie's in trouble!' she cried. 'Coyote!'

Shock rooted Kirstie to the spot. She heard her friend's cries, but the creature's white fangs seemed to mesmerize her. She couldn't move, couldn't defend herself as it crouched above her head, ready to leap.

It snarled and launched itself, flying through the air in a rush of grey and fawn fur; would have landed on top of her, its teeth snapping and tearing, if it hadn't been for Rocky. The horse's head went up, he pulled at the half-tied rope and broke free. Then he whirled round to rear up between the coyote and Kirstie, so that the dog-like creature came down on his back, across the saddle. The sudden movement knocked the coyote sideways on to the ground at Rocky's feet, where it lay winded.

'Don't move!' Hadley ordered Kirstie, seeing what had happened and running from the overhang with Lisa. 'Let the horse handle it!'

She felt her legs shake, her heart beat fast. Rocky had reared up again, he was intent on bringing his hooves down on the coyote, which rolled clear at the last instant. The mustang reared again, the wild dog writhed and staggered to its feet. Tail between

its legs, head hanging, it crept away before the flailing hooves landed a second time.

Then Hadley was there, taking hold of Rocky's tether, making sure that the coyote had had enough and really was on its way. He watched it slink into the brushwood in the shadow of the rocks.

'How's Rocky? Is he OK?' Kirstie came to all of a sudden, as if a hypnotist had clicked his fingers and released her from a spell. Shock made her body tremble from head to foot.

The old wrangler held him tight, checked his back and haunches for scratches and bites. 'There's not a mark on him,' he confirmed.

'God, you were lucky!' Lisa gasped.

Kirstie shook her head. 'Not lucky. It was down to Rocky. He saved me!'

She leaned weakly against him, stroking his neck while he lowered his head and turned towards her.

'Sure thing,' Hadley agreed. He pulled his hat low over his forehead and gave no other sign that a crisis had been narrowly avoided all the time they were at Bear Hunt Overlook, nor during the ride back to the ranch. It was only when they were unsaddling the horses in the corral and Sandy Scott hurried over to find out how Rocky had coped with his first trail ride that the wrangler let anything slip.

He was taking the bay stallion's heavy saddle from Kirstie and carrying it into the tack-room when he crossed paths with the anxious ranch owner.

'Well?' Sandy demanded.

Kirstie watched Hadley's face. She held her breath and prayed for him to give the right answer. The old man's narrowed eyes and straight, thin-lipped mouth gave nothing away.

'You got yourself a good horse,' he said at last with the ghost of a smile. 'He's worth every cent you paid.'

8

'OK, we can relax!' Matt announced. He came off the phone with good news for Sandy. 'I've been speaking with a guy called Jerry Santos. He's staying with his wife and three kids at Lone Elm Trailer Park. Lennie told him about this place and now he wants to book a cabin and a riding holiday for the whole family, starting tomorrow!'

It was a week after Kirstie had started riding Rocky out on the trails, when the mustang had first won Hadley's approval. Ever since the day with the coyote, the old wrangler had insisted on taking horse and rider out with his advanced group to show Rocky the most difficult rides and to test out his temperament to the limit. As a further test, both the head wrangler and Charlie had also ridden him. So far, so good, Hadley had reported to his boss. The bay horse had taken every overlook, every cascading waterfall, each challenge that the mountain trails provided easily in his stride.

As yet, there had been no decision to put a guest rider in Rocky's saddle, but confidence in him was growing. Kirstie felt that it wouldn't be long now before the ex-rodeo horse became a full working member of the Half-Moon Ranch team.

And now the cash flow problem caused by Sandy's impulse buy seemed to be easing too. Extra, last-minute guests recommended by Lisa's grandfather would bring in much-needed money, and even Matt was smiling as he gave them the news.

'Great! So we get to keep Yukon and her foal?' Kirstie walked out of the house with her brother and mom, passing the round pen as they made their way to the corral. Inside the fenced ring, the tiny, coal-black horse skipped and pranced in the early sun.

Sandy nodded, then paused. 'Time to give her a name?' she suggested. It was all the answer Kirstie needed.

Stepping on the bottom rung of the fence, she leaned in and smiled at the foal's antics and at Yukon contentedly nipping hay from a net on the far side of the pen. 'Your turn to choose,' she said to Matt.

'A name for the foal?' He was still checking figures in his head, not concentrating on the high kicks and wobbles, the dancing and prancing of the youngster. 'You choose,' he told Kirstie absentmindedly, then walked on.

Just then, the little horse tried out a kick with her back legs. She churned up a cloud of dust in the sandy pen. The dust got into her nose, she shook her head and sneezed.

'Pepper,' Kirstie decided with a broad grin. 'From now on, that's her name!'

'*All* the horses can stay!' she told Lisa the next morning.

While Matt and Sandy were busy with the usual Sunday transfer of guests from the ranch to Denver airport, the girls had decided to ride out along

Meltwater Trail to Miners' Ridge. It was a chance for a quiet, peaceful trek without having to think about visitors or stick closely to the trails.

'For a while back there, I was afraid things weren't working out,' Kirstie confessed. They'd reached the ridge, with Dead Man's Canyon below and a track up through the ponderosa pines to Lisa's grandfather's trailer park. Rocky took the ridge without faltering, despite the steep drop to one side. He looked keenly at the grassed-over mounds of waste rock from the old goldmine, decided they were OK, and walked steadily on. Not even the rush of water over the rocks and the loud, foaming cascade into the canyon put him off, as Kirstie led the way.

'I knew Rocky would make the grade!' Lisa said cheerfully. 'Thanks to you, of course!'

'And to Charlie.' Kirstie reminded her of the young wrangler's help. She breathed deeply and relaxed in the saddle as they left the ridge behind. 'How about calling in on your grandpa?' she suggested.

'Sure.' Lisa brought Lucky up alongside Rocky, and for a while they walked without talking. Their silence brought out the mule deer from the bushes and long, dry grass which grew on the open slopes. The slender, large-eared deers wandered by in groups of five or six, the cautious doe leading her fawns and year-old young to better grazing land below the ridge.

'Lennie made Matt's day yesterday,' Kirstie told Lisa, once they reached the more level, broader track that led to Lone Elm. 'He's sending some people from the trailer park to the ranch. Matt's had dollar signs in his eyes all morning!'

Lisa grinned. 'I heard that. Grandpa says the Santos family drove all the way down from New Jersey in a big recreational vehicle to take their vacation in the Rockies. But I guess they've had it up to here with roughing it. Now they want a week in a nice cabin with a fireplace and a porch, and someone to do the cooking and the dishes!'

'That sounds good to me too!' Kirstie laughed. Up ahead, she could already see the entrance to the trailer park, and beyond that the neat log-built reception building nestled under the tall, solitary elm tree from which the park took its name.

'Hey, that could be Jerry Santos and co moving out right now!' Lisa spotted a high-sided, silver motor home parked by the side of the office. It gleamed in the sunlight; a giant vehicle decked out with big steel fenders, ladders on to the roof, windows with fancy blinds. In the cab sat a woman and three small kids, and down by the office door stood a man in T-shirt and shorts. 'Let's go see!'

Quick off the mark, Lucky broke into a trot and then a lope along the smooth track. Less eager to break the peaceful spell of their mountain ride, Kirstie held Rocky back for a few seconds. She saw more deer and stopped to watch a buck rub his beautiful antlers against a pine tree, listening to the scrape and hollow rattle of horn against bark. In the undergrowth behind, a young, pale brown doe with huge, dark eyes darted from bush to bush.

Glancing ahead, Kirstie saw that Lisa and Lucky had already reached the entrance to the trailer park. She decided to give Lisa time to say hello to her grandpa before she caught them up. But then she frowned. The fair-haired man in shorts was stepping towards the silver motor home and climbing up into the cab as Lisa arrived. He was turning on the engine. The giant vehicle was starting to move out of the park.

'Lisa, watch out for Lucky!' Kirstie yelled. Her voice was drowned by the engine.

And now she had other things to worry about. The motor home crawled through the exit, beneath the overhead sign that Lennie Goodman had erected only that spring. Thirty feet long, reflecting the sun's rays, engine growling, it advanced on to the track.

'For God's sakes!' she muttered. Didn't the driver have enough sense to wait until she and Rocky had ridden by? Though broader than the steep mountain trails, the road couldn't take both motor home and horse. And anyway, Rocky was beginning to play up.

He saw the square front of the tall cab, the gleaming metal grille, the flash of sunlight reflected on glass, the movement of passengers inside. For a few moments, Rocky stood stock still.

Kirstie tightened the reins. 'Back up!' she whispered. If Rocky would pull back a few feet, she could guide him up a side track, out of the way of the slowly advancing motor home. 'Come on, Rocky, let's get out of here!'

No way was the driver going to stop, she realised. Maybe he thought he had the right of way in his huge motor home, and expected a mere horse and rider to automatically give way. Or maybe he just didn't realise he was giving her a problem. In any case, he kept right on coming.

She felt the mustang flinch. Instead of backing to safety, he chose to advance with edgy, uneven strides. Kirstie pulled on the reins. 'Come on, Rocky, what's going on?' Why wouldn't he do as he was told?

He stopped. His head was up, ears flat; the old, angry signs. And every muscle was tense, every nerve on edge as he skittered across the dirt road, defying the oncoming driver.

The man at the wheel must have seen the horse by now. He was a hundred yards away and still creeping forwards. Either he was mean or stupid. 'Stop!' Grasping the reins in one hand, Kirstie made a firm signal with the other.

No response. The giant vehicle kept on coming. There was a roar, a cloud of black fumes from the exhaust, a swing off the road into the gravel and brushwood, as if the driver had momentarily lost control. A screech of brakes, the churn of loose stones under the massive wheels; the inexperienced driver fought to bring the tilting motor home back on to the level.

'Easy, boy!' Kirstie knew deep down that she was

losing him. He was ignoring her voice, the touch of the reins. His muscles were bunched, his head straining. Still she tried to get him back.

But it was no good. With a toss of his head, Rocky rested back deep on to his haunches, then threw himself forward in a terrific buck. Kirstie flew with him in a high arc, grabbing the saddle horn as she went, legs flying from the stirrups, head jerked back in a sudden whiplash movement. Her hat flew off, her hair fell loose as she clung to the saddle and felt Rocky's back feet land with a thudding jolt.

It was then, much too late, that the driver must have realised she was in deep trouble. He put his foot on the brake and trundled to a halt. The motor home hissed, spouted out blue smoke, then sat motionless astride the track.

With Kirstie still clinging tight, trying to slide her feet back into the stirrups and regain hold of the reins, Rocky arched his back and stamped his feet. A huge fear had him in its grip. His head went up again, his mane whipping against her arms. Then he reared and twisted, throwing her back and sideways. She held on, felt the bunched fury of his muscles.

Then there were footsteps running down

the road, two figures appeared from behind the stationary motor home. Kirstie glimpsed Lisa and Lennie Goodman coming to help. But Rocky spun away, rearing once, twice, three times. She was flung backwards and forwards, biting her tongue hard as her jaw fell open then snapped shut with the violent rise and fall. There was blood in her mouth; a salty, metallic taste, but no time to feel pain.

The mustang whirled, turned and reared. It was the wild Rocky; the frightened, crazy Rocky of the rodeo. An old fear had exploded in his brain, making him fight to be rid of his rider, to rage up the mountain to freedom once more.

'Hang on, Kirstie!' Lisa cried.

She gripped the horn, pressed her legs against the mustang's flanks, her head jerked this way and that. Already dizzy and weak, she felt him veer to the side and charge at the steep slope that bordered the road. There was a boulder in his path that he would smash against unless he took off and jumped ... she soared with him and landed, felt him thunder on up the rough hillside.

Rocky had jumped clear of the road and charged on up the steep slope, between trees and rocks, in a mad frenzy to be away from the terrifying, hissing truck. Reins flapping, stirrups crashing against his sides, and with Kirstie slumped forward in the saddle, he raced on.

Tall tree trunks flashed by, branches whipped against her and she cried out. She recognised the ridge that Rocky had reached and the drop into Dead Man's Canyon. There was blood trickling from her mouth, a throbbing sensation as the pain set in. And still she must duck and sway out of reach of the blurred branches, gasp for breath and stay in the saddle . . . not fall . . . not land on the dangerous rocks or be flung over the edge of the cliff down the sheer drop into the canyon . . .

Rocky swerved to avoid a low bush. He stumbled against loose rocks, fell to his knees.

Kirstie felt herself thrown forward so hard that she lost hold of the saddle horn. Rocky was down and she was flying through the air. The world turned and spun. Her shoulder crashed against a rock, there was a shooting pain in her neck and head, then blackness, silence . . . nothing.

'Kirstie . . .? Come on, wake up! Kirstie . . . please!'

She came round from a dim, distant world, out

of a dark tunnel, away from the silent shadows. She opened her eyes to trees, sky, and Lisa's anxious face peering down at her.

'Where's Rocky?' she moaned. Her mouth felt like a dark cave in which the hollow words rolled.

'Never mind the horse. Are you OK?' Lisa knelt by her side, afraid to touch her.

'What happened? Where's Rocky?'

'He threw you off, remember? You landed badly, you've been out cold for more than ten minutes!'

'But where is he?' Struggling to raise herself on to her elbows, she turned her stiff neck to search the empty hillside.

Gently Lisa wiped the blood from her face. 'He threw you then ran off. Grandpa took Lucky and went for help. You lie still until the others get here.'

Kirstie shook her head and struggled to sit up. 'I need to find him. Which way did he go?' But the pain in her shoulder was bad, her head swam and she sank back down.

'Forget about Rocky,' Lisa whispered. 'You're hurt. You're not going anywhere.'

The trees shook their golden leaves down on her.

They floated and drifted on to her face. She felt their feathery touch . . .

'Kirstie?' Lisa's echoing voice broke through.

Her eyelids fluttered open again. *Forget about Rocky*. That was Lisa. *He threw you, then ran off. Forget about Rocky. Forget about him* . . . She tried to focus on the trees over her head, but she heard the beat of hooves on rock, saw a dream-horse race along the ridge. *Forget about Rocky*. That's what they would all say when they got here, her mom, Hadley, and Matt. *He's a problem horse. He'll never be any good*.

Their voices floated in her head. It throbbed and spun. The voices judged the mustang and sentenced him over and over again: *Forget him*. From now on, she knew that this was how it would be.

9

The doctor came from San Luis and reassured Sandy Scott that Kirstie's shoulder was badly bruised but not broken. The cut on her tongue would also heal itself in time.

It wasn't the cuts and bruises that mattered. Forced to lie in bed while her mom showed the doctor downstairs, Kirstie dismissed the minor injuries she'd sustained when Rodeo Rocky threw her and fled up the mountain. What mattered was the damage to her dream that one day soon he would join the team of horses at Half-Moon Ranch.

She stared out of the open window at distant Eagle's Peak, nursing her shattered pride and hope.

'It could've been worse, I guess.' Lisa slid quietly into the room while the grown-ups talked over the accident in the ranch-house kitchen. 'No broken bones.'

'Have they found Rocky?' Kirstie demanded.

'Your mom sent Hadley and Charlie out to look.' Gazing awkwardly at the floor, Lisa found it hard to meet her friend's intense gaze.

'But they didn't find him yet?' She realised the runaway stallion could have travelled miles off the trails and beaten tracks into thick pine forests, or even above the snowline into the icy wastes of the high peaks of the Meltwater range.

'Nope. They took a two-way radio, so they'll call as soon as they've got news.' Lisa glanced up and tried to smile. 'How are you doing?'

'Fine.' Kirstie stared hard at Lisa's flushed face.

'I heard the doc tell your mom you had to stay in bed in case you got concussion.'

'I'm fine! It's Rocky I'm worried about.' Kirstie felt a long, embarrassed pause develop between them. 'Do you know something you're not telling me?'

'Nope.' Lisa's colouring was pale and freckled. When she lied, her face flushed bright red.

Kirstie sat up in bed, trying to catch snatches of conversation from downstairs. 'What's going on down there? What are they saying?'

'I dunno. Grandpa's telling your mom about the accident. He reckons Rocky went kind of crazy back there and you're lucky you weren't hurt real bad.'

'Is that right?' She was all for getting straight out of bed and running down to the kitchen to put them right, until Lisa put out a hand to stop her.

'Wait till they've calmed down. Arguing won't do any good right now.'

So Kirstie sat on the edge of the bed and gave her friend a rough time instead. 'It's not Rocky who was crazy; it's that dumb driver! What on earth was he thinking; driving a giant truck at a horse like that? Doesn't he *know* that's the best way to spook any horse on this planet? Let alone one that's been through what Rodeo Rocky's been through!'

'You don't need to tell me!' Lisa pointed out when Kirstie at last paused for breath.

'Look, how can they blame Rocky? To him that motor home sure as hell looked like the truck they used to drive him down from Wyoming in! Big steel

fenders, wide, flashing windscreen, loud engine . . .'
To Kirstie it was obvious. 'Rocky sees this monster
machine coming down the track towards him, and
he thinks, no way! Once was enough. He's not
gonna stick around until men with ropes come and
grab him again. He's been there before!'

'Sure, Kirstie, I hear what you're saying.' Going
to look out of the window at the doctor's car driving
out under the Half-Moon Ranch sign, Lisa tried
once more to get a word in. 'And maybe you're
right about Rocky having a good reason not to like
these giant trucks, but . . .'

'*But*, nothing!' She felt her heart pounding with
a fierce desire to defend the horse. 'Rocky was only
doing what any horse in his right mind would have
done!'

Lisa sighed, opened her mouth to speak, then
changed her mind.

'Go ahead!' Nursing one elbow in the palm of
her hand to ease the pain in her shoulder, Kirstie
joined her at the window. She winced and frowned
to see the very motor home they'd been talking
about parked on a flat piece of land beyond the
bridge over the creek. It looked like the Santos
family had arrived for their week's stay at the ranch.

The sight of it made her stomach churn. 'OK, Lisa, give it to me straight.'

Lisa turned her grey eyes to meet Kirstie's blue ones. 'I guess you have to know.'

'Know what?' She heard the door swing open, saw Matt stride out across the yard, heard her mom's footsteps treading back and forth in the hallway at the bottom of the stairs.

At last Lisa spoke the difficult words. 'Sandy's gonna blame Rocky, whatever you say. It figures. She's real worried about you. And if Grandpa tells her the horse went crazy, no way is she gonna let you ride him again . . .!'

'Not let me ride Rocky?' The idea struck Kirstie like a physical blow.

Lisa chewed her lip and nodded. 'You'd better believe it,' she murmured. 'And that's even if they do track him down and get him back to Half-Moon Ranch!'

'I swear, Mom, it won't happen again!' Kirstie pleaded like she'd never pleaded before.

It was Monday morning, before the wranglers set off from the corral with the groups of new visitors. Hadley and Charlie had returned empty-handed the night before, reporting that there was no sign of Rodeo Rocky in any of the predictable places. They'd ridden through Dead Man's Canyon, and as far as Eden Lake, where they knew the runaway stallion would have found good grass for grazing. But there wasn't a hoofmark anywhere to show the path he'd taken.

Now Kirstie was confined to the ranch house to help her get over the accident, and though Lisa had promised to call and keep her company, a long, empty day stretched ahead.

'Give me a guarantee.' Sandy spoke quietly but firmly. 'Give me a one hundred per cent promise that, suppose we do track him down and bring him back, Rocky is gonna be a safe ride!'

Kirstie took a sharp breath through her nose. She tried to frame the words, to explain that the incident with the motor home had been a one-off.

In the tense silence, Sandy turned away. 'You can't. Nobody can.'

Kirstie stepped across her path, blocking the door before she went out on to the porch to collect her hat and set off on the day's ride. 'Look at it this way. There are no roads here on the ranch land; only trails for horses. So, if Rocky is spooked by trucks because of what he went through earlier this summer, what we do is make sure he doesn't go near any roads. No roads: no trucks, see!' Her voice cracked, her eyes shone with tears as she spread her hands to plead even harder than before. 'No trucks: no problem!'

Sandy shook her head. 'Kirstie, don't!'

'Why not?' To her, it was a life or death issue. No way could they give up on Rocky.

'Because I already made up my mind. It's too risky.' Gently Sandy pushed past and picked up her hat.

'So?' Once more, Kirstie stepped across her path. 'What are you gonna do? Just leave Rocky up there in the mountains?' How long would he survive in the company of dangerous coyotes and mountain lions?

'Nope.' Sandy avoided looking at Kirstie as she put on her stetson and called across the yard to Matt to say that she was on her way. 'As your brother just pointed out, there's two thousand dollars' worth of mustang out there somewhere. Hadley and Charlie will ask the other ranchers for help. There's gonna be a big search party tonight. We'll find him, you bet.'

Kirstie took this in. She should have been relieved, but somehow she wasn't. 'Then what?' she demanded from the top step of the porch. Her mom was striding away, not looking back.

'I called the sale barn in San Luis,' she replied, her voice muffled as she hurried off. 'We send Rocky to the auction at dawn tomorrow!'

'All you have to do is saddle Lucky for me!' Kirstie begged Lisa for help when her friend arrived in her grandpa's pick-up truck. 'I can't lift the weight of it with this shoulder the way it is!'

'No way!' Lisa backed out of the bedroom on to the landing. She put both hands in front of her to ward off Kirstie's pleas.

'Please! I'll do anything you want in return! Just this one little favour, Lisa, *please*!' All morning she'd sat by the bedroom window planning this, waiting for Lisa to show up.

'It's not a little favour, it's a mega, mega one! What's your mom gonna say if I let you do this?' She backed down the stairs shaking her head hard.

'I won't say a word, I promise. Your story is, you got here and I was already gone. The whole thing was down to me!'

'Uh-oh!' Lisa pointed out that Sandy Scott would know there was no way Kirstie could have saddled Lucky alone. 'Besides, I wouldn't do it anyway. It's too risky.'

'Since when did taking a risk become a problem?' Kirstie had struggled into her clothes before Lisa had arrived. Now she was pulling on her boots and following her friend downstairs. 'We always take risks, don't we?'

'The doc said to stay in bed, remember!'

'That was yesterday. That was before I knew they planned to send Rocky to the sale barn!'

Lisa went on backing out across the hallway into the porch. 'OK, so say I saddle Lucky for you. You ride out on a trail looking for Rocky. What then?'

Seeing that she was weakening, Kirstie ran forward and grabbed her eagerly by the arm. 'I made a plan! I'm trusting Lucky to track Rocky down. Lucky has got this kind of thing about him . . . you know, like a . . . connection!'

Slowly Lisa nodded. 'You reckon he'll find him, wherever he ran to?'

'Yeah! Horses can hear and smell way, way better than we can. And Lucky's smart. He thinks like

Rocky thinks; kind of wild and clever. It won't take him long.'

'Ouch!' Lisa pulled her arm away. 'Then what?' she demanded.

'Then . . .' Kirstie hesitated. This was the part of the plan she wanted to keep to herself. 'You don't want to know, Lisa. You really don't want to know!'

'If you don't tell me, no way will I help you!' Hurt that Kirstie wouldn't confide in her, Lisa drew back.

Kirstie's shoulders sank, she sighed. 'Let's just say it's something I've gotta do.'

'So Rocky doesn't get sent to the auction?' Lisa frowned and stared hard at Kirstie's troubled face.

As she nodded, she felt hot tears come to her eyes. 'It's gonna break my heart, believe me.'

'And it's secret?' Lisa whispered.

Another nod. She brushed the tears away and held her head up. 'Trust me, Lisa.'

There was a long, long silence. Then the red-haired girl broke away and across the yard towards the bridge. 'Wait here,' she yelled over her shoulder as she broke into a run. 'You go to the tack-room. I'll bring Lucky in from the meadow!'

Kirstie was breaking every rule there was to break.

The doc had said no riding for a few days, and here she was taking Lucky out along Meltwater Trail. Her mom had told her to give up on the problem rodeo horse, and that was something she just wasn't ready to do.

Giving up on Rocky and sending him in a dark horse-box along the rough road to San Luis was the worst kind of betrayal. Worse than death for the wild, free-spirited stallion.

And Kirstie loved that horse. She loved him for his copper-coated beauty, his strength and willpower, and because of the way he'd learned to trust.

So she followed the track by waterfalls and fast-running streams, through Fat Man's Squeeze to Miners' Ridge, to the point where she and Lisa had left the official trail and bushwhacked over to the trailer park the day before.

Lucky took it easy, his trot smooth and gentle, as if he knew that Kirstie's shoulder hurt and this was the reason she sat stiff in the saddle, trusting him to pick his way through trees and rocks.

'Your mom will never forgive me if anything bad happens,' Lisa had whispered as she'd tacked Lucky up and helped Kirstie into the saddle. Her face had been pale and strained as she'd stood by the corral fence and watched her leave.

Kirstie had managed to smile back at her. 'You weren't even here!' she'd murmured.

And now she and Lucky had reached the spot where the Santos's motor home had spooked Rocky. There were the tyre-marks up ahead, where Jerry Santos had driven the giant vehicle off the track, and here were the scuffs and hoofprints where Rocky had reared and bucked. His track led across the dirt road, over a jagged rock and on up the hill.

Setting Lucky to follow the trail, Kirstie glanced over her shoulder to check that there was no one around. One way was the entrance to Lennie Goodman's trailer park. In the other direction was the empty road she'd just travelled. For a moment she felt Lucky hesitate and flick his ears as if he'd picked up a sound. Was it Rocky? Was the runaway horse standing quietly in that dark clump of pine trees, or behind that tall rock? Kirstie urged the palomino to investigate.

But no; that was too much to hope. The noise that had alerted Rocky must have been a deer or even a mountain lion. A cougar stalking through the bushes would make the palomino pay attention, that was for sure.

So Kirstie turned him away from possible danger and took a track away from the trailer park towards Eden Lake, high in the mountains.

This was a hunch worth following, but only a hunch. The lake, at eight thousand feet, was surrounded on three sides by massive rock-faces. It was a natural cul-de-sac, but the approach provided plenty of good grass on the open slope. Rocky would find food, water from the crystal clear lake, and shelter from the wind in the lee of the mountains. Instinct might have led him there for the night.

Lucky too seemed to think it was a good decision. He picked up his pace as they left behind the last signs of civilisation; a trailer nestling in the pine trees at the edge of the trailer park. His head was up, he was wanting to lope, but Kirstie held him back because cf the pain in her shoulder. She would keep him to a trot, posting out of the saddle to cut down the jarring sensation of the sitting trot.

They were cutting across country, about to cross the Eden Lake trail, and Kirstie was looking around to check that Hadley's group was nowhere in sight, when Lucky suddenly skittered sideways, then stopped. He'd heard or seen something unusual, or else he'd picked up his rider's unease and the slightest thing had begun to spook him. 'Come on, this isn't your problem,' she said softly.

Lucky ignored her. He listened, turned his head down the trail, waited.

Then Kirstie heard the sound of hooves coming along the trail. One horse only; approaching fast up the slope. Kirstie frowned and urged Lucky on into the covering of some nearby trees and rocks. Still he refused.

Then the horse rounded a bend and came into view. He was pale in the shadow of an overhanging rock, striding out so that his tail streamed behind him. His rider ducked to avoid a low branch, and when she sat up, her hat flew back to reveal dark red curls.

'Lisa!' Kirstie called out. She reined Lucky round and went to meet her friend. 'What the . . .?'

Lisa drew level, then pulled Cadillac up. 'So?' she demanded, challenging Kirstie before she had time to object. 'No way was I gonna let you ride up here by yourself!'

'You've been following me!' This explained the

noises in the bushes by the trailer park; Lucky's edginess.

'Yep.' Lisa studied Kirstie's face. 'You look pretty bad. How's the shoulder? No, don't answer that.' She stared harder than ever. 'So, where are we going?'

'We?' At first, Kirstie wouldn't show how glad she was to see Lisa. Finding Rocky was something she alone had to do. Yet she acknowledged the flood of relief she'd felt when she'd recognised both horse and rider. And she knew she didn't have the heart to send them back.

'*We*. You, me, Lucky and Cadillac.' Lisa leaned forward to pat her horse's smooth, cream neck. Then she glanced up at Kirstie with a warm smile. 'So, don't give me a hard time, OK? Where you go; me and Cadillac, we go too!'

All morning they criss-crossed the wooded slopes, searching for the runaway horse. Lucky and Cadillac took the steep hills in their stride, pushing ahead to Eden Lake past creeks and waterfalls, across fast-running streams and up to clearings in the forest where Kirstie and Lisa could ride out on to flat overlooks to scan the valleys for signs of movement.

Beneath them, the land was empty and still. Once they caught a distant glimpse of one of the trail-riding groups; a string of horses taking their riders along the beginners' Five Mile Creek Trail. Another time, a movement just below their overlook turned out to be a small family of mule deer. Kirstie swallowed her disappointment and headed on to the pasture by the lake.

As they drew near, the sun was high overhead and the heat building up. The sky was a dense blue, there was no breeze. The girls rode into the bowl of land where the clear lake spread before them, into a world of green and blue silence.

Please! Kirstie prayed as she rode Lucky across the lush pasture towards the lake. *Even if Rocky isn't here, please give us a clue!*

A blue jay took off from a nearby tree and squawked across the sparkling water. High overhead, a golden eagle soared on the wind currents.

Riding ahead, Lisa took Cadillac to the water's edge to let him drink. 'Hey!' she called. 'Kirstie, come look at these prints!'

Rocky had been to Eden Lake. The solo prints of hooves in the mud proved it. He wasn't here now;

the great bowl of rocks was empty except for the birds. But he had visited the spot.

'How long ago?' Lisa asked.

'Not long. The track's fresh.' Kirstie had dismounted to crouch beside the water. Lucky stood nearby, watching, listening.

'The prints head across the pasture towards that creek.' From the vantage point of her saddle, Lisa pointed to more prints in the soft grass.

A stream flowed out of Eden Lake, across the flat plateau towards a sudden drop. Kirstie recognised Crystal Creek and Falls as a sight that took visitors' breath away when they first saw it from the trail below.

She also remembered that Hadley always gave a warning for them to stay well clear of the tumbling, foaming mass of water that slid over the edge and crashed between the rocks. Though it looked cool, clear and inviting, the creek had strong currents and dangerous banks. A horse tempted to drink there could easily lose his footing in soft, quicksand-like soil, then be dragged into the current and swept away.

Frowning to discover that Rocky had chosen such a risky refuge, Kirstie remounted Lucky and began to ride towards the creek. The aspen trees on the far bank whispered gently in the breeze from the ice-capped peaks. The light danced on their silvery leaves and dappled the shaded ground.

'Hey!' Lisa said softly. She pointed to the shadowy bank.

Lucky stopped in the bright sunshine amidst a sweep of green grass and blue columbines. Kirstie stared into the rippling shadows. There was a copper glint, a horse emerging from the trees. Bay and black, with the strange metallic tint. Head up, raising himself on to his hind legs and whinnying loudly, Rocky greeted Kirstie from the far bank of Crystal Creek.

10

'What now?' Lisa's question was high and tense.

Kirstie drank in the sight of the magnificent mustang. As if in a daze, she rode Lucky towards the creek.

Lisa followed. 'Come on, Kirstie, what's the plan?'

She stopped at the water's edge. The creek ran fast and deep. Not far to their left, it disappeared over a narrow ledge of rock in a thundering roar.

'So, we found him!' Lisa begged Kirstie to stop and explain. 'You can't take Rocky back to the ranch, so what are we gonna do?'

'*Me*,' she replied. 'What am *I* gonna do? By myself. Alone.'

Rocky came towards them and stood on the far bank, separated only by the creek.

'Kirstie, for God's sake!' Lisa could see she was in pain. Her face was pale, her jaw clenched as she let go of Lucky's reins and eased her shoulder.

Taking a deep breath, with her eyes still on Rocky, she answered quietly and firmly. 'The plan's real simple. I get up on Rocky and head him way out of here into the mountains. I ride him to Eagle's Peak and down into the next valley, where there are no ranches, no roads; just miles of forest.'

'And?' Lisa rode Cadillac tight up beside her, following her gaze across the water to where Rocky stood.

'And nothing,' Kirstie said. It was wild land without fences, with vast stretches of grass between the trees; pastures where deer grazed and horses roamed. Like Wyoming. Like the land the mustang knew best. She took a deep breath and told Lisa what was in her heart. 'I'm gonna set Rocky free!'

'But first you have to cross the creek!' Lisa pointed out the most obvious difficulty. 'Forget that the pain in your shoulder is killing you. Ignore the fact that your mom is relying on getting her two grand back on the horse . . .'

'Don't think I haven't thought it through a hundred times.' Kirstie shook her head and began to look for a safe place to cross. 'But hey, have you got a better idea?'

The question silenced Lisa. She frowned and walked Cadillac slowly along the bank of the stream. Opposite, Rocky had broken into an agitated trot. He ran a short distance by the water's edge, away from Crystal Falls, turned quickly and trotted back.

'OK, Lucky, we need to join Rocky.' Kirstie edged her horse into the cold current. She felt him flinch as water lapped his knees. He hesitated, looking at Rocky, who was still trotting and wheeling round, whinnying now and pawing the ground.

'How deep is that water?' Lisa asked nervously. She watched a piece of sodden driftwood speed by, tumbling between jagged rocks, then swirling and disappearing under the surface.

Kirstie pressed Lucky's sides to order him on. 'It doesn't matter; he can swim it, no problem.'

'In that current?'

'He's strong. He can make it.' She glanced across

the creek. It was thirty feet wide at this point, and the far bank was low and flat enough for her horse to climb out easily. Only, Rocky seemed to be growing more upset at the place she'd chosen and to be warning Lucky against it. The mustang stamped and snorted, wheeled away and raced upstream. He took a slope and stopped on a ridge of rock, inviting them to follow.

With Lucky still only knee-deep in the water, Kirstie narrowed her eyes. 'No, that's no good. It's too steep for us to get out there.' Her chosen place was better, she decided. Once more she gave Lucky the signal to plunge in deep.

Reluctantly, straining at the reins, the palomino obeyed. He walked awkwardly into the current until, with a sudden jerk he was out of his depth and swimming. The water rose around Kirstie's legs and swamped the saddle. It closed over Lucky's shoulders. His legs paddled smoothly and strongly, resisting the force of the rushing current, carrying them across the creek to the far shore.

The ice-cold water pushed against Kirstie's legs. She was waist-deep and still in the saddle, leaning into the current to resist it, struggling with the pain of her injured shoulder. But Lucky was making progress; they'd gone beyond the halfway point and the bank was now only a short way off. Rocky had charged down from the ridge and stood quivering on a ledge of black rock some fifteen feet from the grassy spot where Lucky would land. He was still agitated; his ears were back, he tossed his head and stamped. Then, as Lucky found his feet touching the river bed again, there was a sudden swirl and giant eddy. The current had switched. It threw Kirstie sideways, so that she had to cling to the drenched saddle horn to regain her balance.

'Hang on, Kirstie!' Lisa yelled from behind.

Up ahead, Rocky stopped his restless stamping and froze.

Kirstie hauled herself upright. 'OK!' she whispered to Lucky. The worst was over. He could steady himself and walk on.

One step, two steps; unsteady because of the dangerous current, the palomino emerged from the creek. Three steps. The bed of the stream was strewn with hidden rocks. Lucky staggered. On the black ledge, Rocky reared up, wheeled away, came closer to the spot where Lucky was headed.

Breathless now with the effort of hanging on, dizzy from the rush and swirl of the current, Kirstie willed her horse forward. He rose out of the creek on to the grassy bank.

'Good boy, you made it!' There was a split second when she leaned forward to pat him. A moment when he lifted his first hoof and planted it on the reedy, squelching surface. The hoof sank into mud. It vanished. The soil oozed and sucked it under. Lucky tipped forward, lifted his other front leg, planted it on the bank. It too sank knee-deep.

The horse was up to his knees in soft grey mud. He sank quickly to his shoulders, throwing Kirstie forward out of the saddle, over his head and on to the bank. She let go of the reins, rolled away, felt the mud suck at her, kept on rolling until she could reach out and catch at the stirrup of the saddle Rocky was still wearing. The mustang stood just close enough, at the very edge of the treacherous swamp. He held firm as she rolled and caught the stirrup, took her weight, dragged her clear.

But Lisa was crying out a warning that Lucky was still sinking. She crouched on the far bank, ignoring two figures who'd ridden across the flat meadow from the direction of Eden Lake and were flinging themselves out of their saddles at the water's edge. 'Kirstie, get a rope around Lucky's neck, quick as you can! He's going under! For God's sake, do it!'

Without thinking, Kirstie staggered to her feet and unhitched the lead-rope coiled and hitched to the side of Rocky's saddle. As she ran back to the edge of the swamp, she tied a noose in one end. Then she aimed the rope and threw.

Eight or ten feet away, the palomino strove to keep his head and shoulders clear of the mud, which sucked and oozed at him, dragging him down. His eyes rolled wildly, he lashed his head from side to side, but his feet found nothing solid and his struggles only made him sink more quickly.

The noose landed wide of the palomino. Kirstie groaned and drew the rope back, gathered it and aimed again. This time, it snaked through the air and over Lucky's head.

'Neat!' a voice called from the far bank.

Kirstie glanced up, had time to recognise Hadley and Charlie as the figures who had raced across the meadow. Now Hadley was yelling instructions.

'Tighten the rope!'

She nodded and stepped back until it was taut.

'OK, now tie the end around Rocky's saddle horn!' The wrangler gave smooth, clear orders. 'Done that?'

With trembling, muddy fingers, she did as she was told.

'So, take the bay's reins and lead him!'

She nodded, seeing what the plan was. Rocky was to take the strain of the rope attached to Lucky. He was to walk away from the bank, accepting the weight, easing the palomino clear. But could he, *would* he do it?

She took the reins. 'Walk on, Rocky!' she murmured.

Back in the muddy swamp, Lucky had stopped fighting. He lay helpless, covered in mud and unrecognisable, waiting for rescue.

'Easy, boy!' Kirstie breathed instructions at the strong bay horse. 'I know you warned us not to cross the creek, and you were right. So now it's down to you to save Lucky. Come on, Rocky, pull!'

The mustang understood exactly what was needed. He turned his back on the creek and took the strain. Every muscle in his body tensed, ready to heave. There was a dead weight behind, and silence from the spectators on the opposite bank. The only sound was of mud sucking and oozing around Lucky's exhausted body as Rocky pulled on the rope.

Seconds ticked by. The wet rope creaked. Nothing moved.

'It's no good! It's too tight around Lucky's neck!' Kirstie cried. She realised that the noose would cut into him and choke him.

'Wait!' It was Charlie's turn to come up with an idea. Running for a second rope, he unhitched one from Moose's saddle and brought it back to the creek. He aimed the noose at Lucky, swung it high above his head and threw. The loop hooked around the mud-caked saddle horn.

'Yes!' Kirstie hissed. She held out her hands to catch Charlie's end of the rope. 'Now throw!'

The young wrangler sent the new rope whizzing across the creek. Kirstie caught with her good arm and wound it round Rocky's saddle. With two ropes secure, she ordered the bay horse forward once more.

And by this time Lucky seemed to have regained the energy to help himself. He found firm rock beneath his back feet and pushed. His front legs thrashed through slime and mud, the ropes tightened as Rocky eased forward.

'Pull!' Kirstie whispered, her hand on the mustang's sweating neck.

He inched away from the bank, raised Lucky out of the swamp slowly, steadily.

'Some horse!' Charlie whistled his admiration as the strong stallion pulled.

'Don't let him give up!' Lisa urged.

Hadley stood silently watching the mustang tug the palomino to safety.

With a steadying hand on Rocky's shoulder, feeling his steely willpower concentrated on the act of rescue, Kirstie felt sure he would succeed. All she had to do was trust and wait.

The surface of the grey mud was smooth once more. There was nothing to signal the life and death struggle except trampled reeds by the bank of the creek.

On one side of Crystal Creek stood a small huddle of people: Lisa, Hadley and Charlie, with Sandy and Matt Scott. Sandy's red Dodge pick-up was parked in the meadow. Moose, Crazy Horse and Cadillac grazed nearby.

'We came as soon as you radioed,' Matt told Hadley.

The wrangler nodded. 'Wasn't nothing you could do,' he muttered. 'But I knew you'd want to be here.'

Sandy broke away and walked down to the bank. She stared anxiously across the water at the figures caked in mud; at Kirstie sitting on the ground, slumped forward and sobbing, at Rocky waiting by her side. 'Hold on!' she called.

Kirstie raised her head and nodded. Mud covered every inch of her body. It had caked on her face, in her hair, plastering it to her skull. It was under her fingernails, inside every seam of her clothes. Wiping her hands on the grass, she dragged her hair back from her face and looked round for Lucky.

Her palomino stood next to the mustang. The ropes that had rescued him were still tied. He too was covered from head to foot in thick mud.

Kirstie's tears were tears of relief. Lucky was alive. Rocky had dragged him clear until his front feet found solid ground. The mustang hadn't let up for a second until the palomino was free of the swamp.

And they were proud tears. No other horse would have done for Lucky what Rocky had done. He was smarter, kinder, more loyal than any horse she knew.

'We're crossing the creek higher upstream!' her mom called. 'It's fine beyond the ridge. We'll be right with you!'

146

Kirstie stood up and went over to stand between Rocky and Lucky. 'You knew that!' she said simply to the bay horse. The mustang's savvy must have shown him the safe crossing place. He'd even tried to warn her about the swamp.

And when the others came to fetch them, carrying blankets to throw over the horses and wrap around Kirstie's shoulders, there were no harsh words, no blame for what Kirstie had done. There was more praise for Rocky from Charlie, who took off his saddle and rubbed him down. There were hugs for Lucky from a relieved Lisa, kind words for Kirstie from her worried mom.

'But what about Rocky?' Kirstie begged. Her dream of freedom for him had sunk beneath the muddy swamp on the bank of Crystal Creek. The dreaded sale barn beckoned. 'He saved Lucky's life. Doesn't that make up for him throwing me?'

Sandy shrugged and smiled. 'That's not the way to look at it, honey, and you know it.'

'What other way is there?'

'With some common sense and savvy,' Matt put in, busy checking both horses for signs of injury.

'Horse-savvy or human-savvy?' Kirstie believed in a horse's instinct, but not what her brother called

147

common sense. She believed that Rocky deserved better than the sale barn and turned to her mom, eyes fierce in his defence.

Sandy hesitated and turned to Hadley. 'The big question is still the same; will Rocky ever be safe for guests to ride?'

Kirstie's gaze fixed on the head wrangler. He glanced at her. 'No,' he said.

She groaned and turned away.

'. . . But,' Hadley went on.

Kirstie swung round. She took a deep breath and listened.

'I always said Rocky's a fine horse. Not a guest horse, but a great mustang all the same.'

Matt finished his inspection of Lucky, untied the ropes that linked him to Rocky, and came round to listen. Sandy stood hands on hips, thinking carefully. Lisa was shoulder to shoulder with Kirstie, waiting for more.

'I ain't about to make a long speech,' Hadley told them. 'All I'm saying is, I can think of a way to use the horse so long as you can keep him out of reach of the roads.'

'Which is?' Sandy said slowly.

'Use him as a staff horse at Half-Moon,' the head

wrangler explained. 'He needs a good rider in the saddle, someone who knows horses, not a dude from the city.'

'Meaning you, Hadley?' Matt thought he saw which way the old ranch hand's thoughts were heading.

'Nope.' He shook his head and glanced round the listening group until his eyes lit on the person he was looking for. 'I was thinking more about young Charlie here.'

'Me?' Charlie let his mouth hang open. His tanned face reddened. 'Are you serious?'

'Yes, of course!' Kirstie saw it in a flash. Charlie was the one who'd helped her with Rocky from the start; the only person who'd shared her faith in the problem horse. 'Great!'

'Charlie?' Matt repeated, as if the thought had never crossed his mind.

'Hmm.' Sandy let it sink in. 'You mean, give Rocky to Charlie to head the trail rides?' She nodded slowly. 'That would leave Moose free for a guest to ride. Yeah, that could work.'

Lisa put her hands to her mouth. She turned away. Why wouldn't someone give the final word?

Kirstie held her breath. She saw Charlie's eyes

light up. Hadley, who never praised anybody, who handed out the orders and went about his business, had just said that Charlie knew horses. That was worth more than a gold medal; more than anything to the junior wrangler. And, as if he had a sense of what was going on, Rocky had leaned forward to push his big, beautiful head over Charlie's shoulder.

'How long have you been thinking this way?' Sandy asked Hadley.

The old man shrugged. 'A couple of weeks.'

'But why didn't you say?' Lisa cried.

But Kirstie didn't care about any of that stuff. She stared at her mom, silently pleading for a decision.

Sandy Scott went up to the bay stallion and pushed his bedraggled, dark mane from his face. 'You want to be Charlie's horse, eh, Rocky?'

The mustang blew gently on her hand. He blinked a couple of times, then nudged Charlie's shoulder.

'. . . OK.' Sandy smiled. 'It's a deal.'

Kirstie closed her eyes. Rocky could stay!

When she opened them again, Hadley was ready to get the horses back to the ranch. He gave Charlie orders to coil ropes, lift saddles. Matt was talking the solution through with Sandy, nodding and smiling. Then he went to help Charlie with his chores.

'Hey, Charlie, you gonna brush the mud off of this palomino when we get back?' Hadley called as he led Lucky upstream to cross the creek.

'Sure!' Charlie ran here and there, a wide grin on his face.

'Hey, Charlie, that bay of yours will need his jabs from the vet if he's gonna stay at the ranch. You gonna call Glen Woodford when we get back?'

'Yep!'

'And get him to check the palomino. And call the sale barn to say we're not bringing the bay in after all. And then there's bits needing cleaning, yards needing raking . . .'

'Yup, yup, yup!' Nothing could take the grin off Charlie's face.

Or wipe the feeling of incredible lightness out of Kirstie's heart. She stood by Crystal Creek looking up into Rocky's eyes. They were a clear, deep hazel, reflecting the light from the sky. They gazed steadily back at her, understanding everything.

Tomorrow she would wake up. Out of the window she would see Red Fox Meadow in the long, dew-laden shadow of Eagle's Peak. She would pick out

Crazy Horse and Cadillac, Moose, Jitterbug and Silver Flash.

Lucky would be standing by the gate waiting for her as usual. At his side, most likely in a patch of early sunlight, she would see the bay coat and black mane of a beautiful stallion. He would glint copper in the rays of the sun. He would be looking up at the ranch house, maybe turn his head to the mountains for a second, then back to the house.

Then Charlie would walk out from the bunkhouse, hat low on his forehead, jacket collar turned up. He would stride to the meadow to fetch his horse. Rocky would see him and trot along the fence to greet him. Charlie would slip on a headcollar and open the gate, lead him out. Horse and man, heading to the corral to start a day's work.

'That's how it's gonna be!' she whispered to Rocky.

The horse nodded in the direction of Lucky and the others heading back to Half-Moon Ranch. He nudged her with his nose: *Come on, let's go*!

Another Hodder Children's book

HORSES OF HALF-MOON RANCH
Johnny Mohawk

Jenny Oldfield

When a guest at the ranch falls from his horse, breaking his arm, he accuses his mount, Johnny Mohawk, of bucking him off. Johnny is a half-Arab stallion and certainly high-spirited, but Kirstie doesn't believe the guest's story. Now the pressure is on Sandy Scott to sell one of Kirstie's all-time favourite horses before he endangers other riders. Can Kirstie prove the guest is lying – and discover the reason why?

Another Hodder Children's book

HORSES OF HALF-MOON RANCH
Gunsmoke

Jenny Oldfield

A school group takes over the ranch for a
week. Kirstie befriends Lacey, a loner
with a natural talent for riding. Besotted
with her horse, a blue roan gelding called
Gunsmoke, Lacey breaks ranch rules and
rides off trail alone. When she fails to
return, Kirstie fears the worst; either Lacey
has had a terrible accident, or she's run
away – unaware that a heavy storm is
brewing . . .

Animal Alert series

HORSES OF HALF-MOON RANCH
Jenny Oldfield

All Hodder Children's books are available at your local bookshop, or can be ordered direct from the publisher. Just tick the titles you would like and complete the details below. Prices and availability are subject to change without prior notice.

Please enclose a cheque or postal order made payable to *Bookpoint Ltd*, and send to: Hodder Children's Books, 39 Milton Park, Abingdon, OXON OX14 4TD, UK.

Email Address: orders@bookpoint.co.uk

If you would prefer to pay by credit card, our call centre team would be delighted to take your order by telephone. Our direct line *01235 400414* (lines open 9.00 a.m.–6.00 p.m. Monday to Saturday, 24 hour message answering service). Alternatively you can send a fax on *01235 400454*.

TITLE		FIRST NAME		SURNAME	
ADDRESS					
DAYTIME TEL:			POST CODE		

If you would prefer to pay by credit card, please complete:
Please debit my Visa/ Access/ Diner's Card/ American Express (delete as applicable) card no:

Signature ....Expiry Date ....
If you would NOT like to receive further information on our products please tick the box. ❐